Dragon Banished

Red Dragon Chronicles

Arisha Grabtchak

Dragon Banished

Copyright © 2021 by Arisha Grabtchak

ISBN 13: 9781736731857

Library of Congress Control Number: 2021939837

Cover Image: Arisha Grabtchak

Cover design © by All Things That Matter Press

Published in 2021 by All Things That Matter Press

This book is dedicated to Arisha, the author. While this is not common, neither is the circumstance of the publication of this book. Arisha passed away in 2016 at the age of 23. She was a very bright, remarkable artist with so many interests in her life. Arisha loved nature and animals, she volunteered at dog shelters and enjoyed horseback riding, she collected seashells from every place she visited and could identify every one of them. Since she was little, Arisha was fascinated by dragons—mysterious powerful creatures from a different world. Not surprisingly, dragons became major characters in her fantasy stories. Being a perfectionist, she was constantly scrutinizing and polishing her manuscripts, hoping to publish the whole series. Unexpected death disrupted Arisha's plans but her family keeps working on realizing her dreams. We could only wish that some things would have happened sooner in her life ...

1 ~ To the Camp

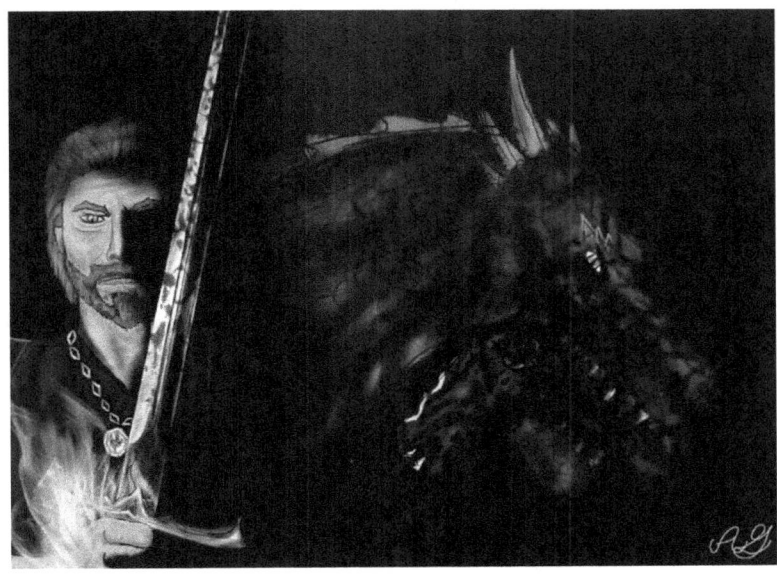

The rest of the trip south passed in a blur. Eiryenne vaguely remembered setting down to rest in snowy valleys and cold and bleak hollows once they'd shaken the last of their pursuers. Danzi only made a stop when he needed a break or Eiryenne needed to eat; usually her stomach gave in before the dragon's wings did.

The farther they flew, the more the landscape began to change. The winds grew warmer, and the biting chill in the air eased as the dragon left winter behind them. Dots of colour started to brighten the drab land as spring began to take hold. It was as if Eiryenne was watching the seasons change at twice their normal speed. The plunge into winter had been sudden because of Tairung's influence, and now it was even stranger to see the snows receding so quickly. Eiryenne had heard the sun was warmer in the southern lands, but this was the first she'd seen of it herself.

She asked Danzi if there was even winter at all where they were going. He replied that there was, but the snows were softer and the freezes shorter. It was a milder climate, but still temperate. "To find the true south," he said, "where hot winds parched the earth for half the year and scalding rains drenched it for the other, one would have to go much farther."

Eiryenne shifted slightly in the dragon's grip as he angled his wings to soar around a craggy mountain. Her sides hurt from being gripped in Danzi's claws for so long. He didn't stop for her to sleep, and she had to take naps midflight.

Still, for the first time since she left her village, Eiryenne was excited. Gone was the threatening dread hanging over her. Now that Tairung was gone, she could do whatever she wanted. She could start living her life in earnest. And what better way to start than to head to the Resistance. From what she'd heard, the legendary force was the only thing that stood against Emperor Varcroft. And after what he had done to her, it would feel good to help some of his other victims.

Danzi slowed as they neared a group of low brown cliffs all set in a row as if it were the gateway to another Firedrake's lair. He paused, slowly beating his wings to hold himself aloft. His golden gaze travelled up and down the stone as if he was searching for something. Or, trying to figure something out. Eiryenne could never be sure what he was looking at; she knew that the dragon could see countless things invisible to the human eye. It could be something as simple as a hidden crack, or as complex as a network of magical illusions. But whatever it was, Eiryenne could see the concentration in Danzi's eyes as he meticulously scanned the rocks. Then, he turned his wings sharply and banked to the left before flying down toward the jagged peaks in a slow spiral.

As they descended, Eiryenne could feel the magic even though she couldn't see it. Danzi glided through layers of hidden spells with every dip of his wings. If she concentrated, she could see the reddish glow of his own magic around his wings, but whatever he was flying through remained impervious to her eyes.

Behind the first row of cliffs were the remains of a mountain, scalloped by some ancient storm. Thin sheets of jagged rock rose from behind the cliffs in narrow rows. Then Danzi flew closer, and arrows glowing with yellow light burst into existence a few feet from them and disappeared just as quickly in a blaze of the dragon's magic. He repelled more arrows and slowed for a landing, aiming for one of the rocky sheets.

As his hind paws reached the rock, Danzi shape-shifted and stood on the rim in his human form. The top of the rocky sheet was less than an inch across, but he balanced on it with ease. The same could not be said for Eiryenne. She tottered precariously on the thin ledge; her arms outstretched for balance.

Danzi put his hand up to blast another arrow out of the air.

The source of the arrows was now clear. As soon as Eiryenne had touched the rock, she saw two archers, one on the same strip of stone as her and Danzi and another on the neighbouring sheet. Both had fresh arrows nocked and aimed.

"Be gone, intruders," shouted the one closest to them. Slimly built and wiry, he had green eyes and a smooth, ageless face. The pointed ears of an elf were visible beneath his mane of silvery hair, and he perched atop the narrow ridge as effortlessly as the fire mage.

The second archer was also an elf but was somewhat bulkier than his companion. He lowered his bow to throw a net of glittering forest-green magic over Danzi, who swept it aside. But while Danzi was distracted, the other archer shifted his bow by the fraction of an inch and shot at Eiryenne.

She didn't even have time to blink, let alone duck, before the arrow was at her face, its cold tip almost touching her forehead. Danzi had grabbed it around the middle.

"Enough." He broke the arrow in half. "I have business with the Resistance. A package to deliver."

Eiryenne's foot slipped, but Danzi grabbed her around the shoulders before she could fall. She took hold of his arm for balance as she regained her footing. The drop in front of her was so steep that it made a chill creep up her spine. Which was silly, really, because she was right next to a dragon. You couldn't be afraid of heights when there was a dragon at your side.

The thinner elf's face was filled with disbelief, but he glanced at his friend as though asking him what they'd do when they ran out of arrows; those clearly weren't working. "A package?"

"Yes," Danzi said. "The one you almost skewered just now. Look, I'm an ally of the Resistance, and I have business at the camp. Let us through, or I'll have to try to break in again. They never like it when I do that."

"What?" The stocky archer blinked. "Who exactly are you? And no lies—"

"New recruits, huh?" Danzi commented. "I didn't know they started sentries so young now. Or so ill-informed. Though I suppose they don't have much choice with the army away. But really, you serve the Resistance, you see a red dragon in the sky, and that doesn't ring a bell? Seriously? Well, perhaps my name will." He paused. "I am Danzi Daggoras."

The silver-haired elf still looked puzzled, but his friend's jaw dropped.

"Ohh," he gasped. "That's the one, that's—"

"What?" The other elf frowned and brushed his hair out of his eyes.

"You know," the stocky elf said, gesturing abstractly. "That's the one—the one that did, y'know, the thing—"

"The thing?" The other elf looked exasperated.

"Y'know, the Kyrahgrun thing."

"No," the thinner one said. "You can't mean *that* fellow. We … oh. Oh …. No wonder our arrows …" He looked at a loss for words.

To her surprise, Eiryenne realized that these two were little more than teenagers. And they realized they were in over their heads.

"We gotta let him through," the stocky elf said. "No choice."

"All right. They can't pin it on us, can they?"

Danzi cleared his throat. "Do all your sentries shoot blindly these days?"

The elf he looked at paled. "Um, we weren't exactly shooting blind." He hesitated. "You were on the kill list, sir. We didn't know your name, but Hurraine put *red dragon* in the 'kill on sight' category."

"Wonderful," Danzi muttered. "Now, if you would just—?"

"Oh, of course." The elves turned to the valley behind them and muttered something. Suddenly the atmosphere around them changed. Eiryenne couldn't quite put her finger on it, but the air seemed clearer, crisper somehow. Not just in the visual sense, but in the magical way as well.

"All clear." The stocky elf gave them a nod and backed away.

Danzi, evidently not trusting Eiryenne's balance any more than she did, kept his grip on her as he transformed. Then he lifted her into the air and took off.

The wind died down as they glided past the last of the cliffs and into the lush valley behind them. Now a forest sprawled out across the land, the trees larger and clustered together more thickly than they had been farther north. Occasionally, Eiryenne would get a glimpse of sunlight reflecting off a spring or pond. But as they came closer, she started to make out low buildings and tents springing into view amidst the trunks.

"Do you always get such a warm welcome?" Eiryenne asked.

"No," Danzi replied. He tipped his wings to quicken the descent. "Usually, they try to kill me *after* they know who I am."

There was a wall circling the camp that hummed with magic, and low towers rose above it every few hundred metres. The buildings beyond it varied from tents to forts to stables stretched along the forest floor and led up to the main fort at the heart of the camp. Eiryenne saw horses grazing in neighbouring meadows. Soon they were low enough to make out individual people. Groups of warriors were training in the various clearings between buildings or trees. Some were doing sword work, others were practicing hand-to-hand combat, and a small group at the back were doing something with flashes of magic.

All activity stopped as Danzi swooped down and landed in a clearing.

Faces turned toward the dragon and the girl as they walked down the row of tents. Some showed outrage, others fear. All were shocked. Eiryenne saw the faces of elves and humans, young and old, as well as various shapeshifters that she couldn't identify. Mixed in with the crowd were other beasts. Some had the head of a bull and a furry body, while others looked like they were half-goat. Eiryenne kept close to the dragon as they made their way into the heart of the camp trying to ignore the hostile stares. After a bit, Danzi shifted into his human form, evidently thinking that might cause less of a stir. Instead, the people surrounding them snapped out of their shocked silence and mobbed them.

"It's him!"

"Daggoras. You traitor!"

"How dare you return."

Swords were unsheathed and bows aimed as angry campers drew level with the newcomers. Danzi stared them down but didn't draw his own weapon.

An elf woman in yellow and white robes pointed her crossbow at Danzi's heart, her thin face severe and blue eyes murderous. "You have some nerve coming back here, dragon."

"Unless you've forgotten, Danzi has nerves of steel." A new voice spoke out over the din of the crowd as a man dressed in flowing, forest-green robes elbowed his way through. He gave Danzi a nod. His expression was surprised, though not displeased. "Welcome back."

"*Welcome?*" burst out one of the bull-men. "He nearly cost us everything. He was banished. And now that he's decided to come back, he will die here." He raised his axe and swung, but Danzi dodged out of the way.

"Calm down," shouted the man in green robes. "This matter will be decided by the Council, like everything else. In the meantime, perhaps you'll let him tell us why he's here."

"I have something to deliver," said Danzi. "Information ... amongst other things." He raised his hand just in time to catch an arrow the elf woman had fired. And now that the stalemate was broken, the other warriors prepared to release their own arrows and spells. Eiryenne realized that this was on the brink of becoming a full-out brawl. Fire flickered along Danzi's sleeves.

"Hold!" Another figure had appeared next to the man in green robes. This one was dressed in a muddy yellow tunic and had a scrunched-up face like he'd spent his days sucking lemons. "I will *not* have this camp burned to the ground again. Riard is right; the Council will decide what to do with him. Back to your usual activities, you lot."

The crowd began to disperse, still muttering angrily. Some of them continued to glare at Danzi. He met each of their gazes; the tension in the air was palpable.

One man took a step forward. He wore a thick, dark tunic with grey breeches and shoulder armour. His beard was long and black, twisted into several braids. There were ornaments carved from bone sitting hanging from his dreadlocks. He gave Danzi a murderous stare.

"I'll kill you myself," he breathed. "My clan will dog your footsteps until the end of your days, dragon. You are the bane of all we stand for, and you will pay for what you've done. Maybe not this moment, this day, but know that your doom is in motion." He paused. "We don't forget, Daggoras. Maybe you do. But we never forget the lives you've destroyed and the suffering that you've caused." He spat on the ground and left.

Danzi slowly let out a breath. "After all I did for these people," he muttered bitterly. "And this is what they think of me now?"

The man called Riard led them past the rest of the tents. Among some of them, Eiryenne caught sight of some girls around her own age. One of them was whispering fervently to the others who were watching her and Danzi pass with their hands over their mouths. A few tents later, she caught sight of a group of young elves. Their expressions varied from surprise to awe, and a blonde boy near the front was gazing at Danzi with open-mouthed wonder.

"I have to say," Riard began. "I never expected to see a red dragon swooping down across the camp again."

Danzi shrugged. "Like I said, I have some things to deliver."

"Tell the Council about it in as much detail as you can afford." He stopped in front of a large, stone-walled building with a sloping roof and opened the door.

Eiryenne followed Danzi inside to see an angled table at the far end of the room that had twelve seats. The sour-faced man in yellow from earlier occupied one of them; he studied Danzi with distaste. Riard took a seat next to him. The other Council members, an assortment of men and women from different species, sat, looking tense. Each wore a brooch with a purple feather over a silver background.

"As Head Councillor, I officially begin this meeting," the man in yellow said. He turned his pudgy face toward Danzi. "Daggoras, report."

Danzi scowled and then began to give them a brief overview of the events that had involved Eiryenne and the Necklace.

While he spoke, Eiryenne let her gaze wander over the tapestry that hung behind the Council's table. At the far left was a lion with golden fur and outstretched wings looking like he was ready to leap off the wall. The weaving was starting to unravel in places, but fresh stitches showed where it had been meticulously repaired. To the right of the lion was another figure, a woman in tan-coloured armour holding a two-pronged sword. The texture around her was slightly different, the material newer and shinier. Between the lion and the woman, a chunk of the tapestry was missing. Charred bits of thread hung around the gap. Either it had once been caught in a fire, or someone really didn't like what that middle part showed.

"So, this girl," the head councillor said, making Eiryenne's thoughts drop back to earth with a thud. "You expect us to just accept her into the camp when she could very well be a spy?"

"Put her through the test if you want to," Danzi replied. "But I can vouch that she isn't."

"Your opinion means *nothing*," burst out the councillor on Riard's left. He narrowed his eyes and looked at Eiryenne. "We *will* test her. Thoroughly. And if there's the slightest *hint* of trouble, she will be beheaded."

Eiryenne gulped.

"But if she's as good a healer as you've described," Riard added quickly. "Then I'm sure she'll make a valuable addition to our team."

"What's your name, girl?" the head councillor asked roughly.

"Um, it's Eiryenne." Eiryenne dared a look up at the rows of angry gazes. To calm herself, she imagined that she was facing a group of twelve horses instead, all lined up in their stalls. Now she found herself wondering whether nameplates would be more useful than those funny brooches they were wearing. "So, Councillor—?"

"Molekk."

"Um, Councillor Molekk. What is this … this test that you were talking about?"

"You shall see." He turned back to Danzi. "As for you, you are now a prisoner of the Council and are entirely at our mercy. So beg for your life, because I highly doubt we'll vote to keep you alive much longer."

"You want to kill me?" Danzi said. "Well, get in line." He swept his gaze around the room. "Because so many have tried. Warriors with far more power at their disposal than any of you have ever had or ever will have. They've all tried very hard, believe me. And all of them have failed. So, take heed of their mistakes." He turned on his heel and swept out of the room, his cloak buffeting the girl as he passed her.

Riard rose from his seat with a piece of parchment in his fist. "Might as well get this over with," he muttered.

"Um, you're going to test me now?" Eiryenne asked.

"Yes. It's not that bad, really." Riard came to a stop in front of her, and Eiryenne was suddenly aware of half a dozen mages' gazes examining her, poking, and prodding at her magic.

Once the Council finished examining her, Molekk scowled. "She's clean." He looked disappointed. "Get on with it, Riard."

Riard looked at the piece of parchment in front of him. "All right, Eiryenne, repeat after me." He squinted at whatever was written on the parchment. "*Ichstemeay ralisteo damerola.*"

"*Ichste … may ralosti damr… ra.*" Eiryenne tried to match the pronunciation, but it was hard.

The councillors seemed to take her struggles as a suspicious sign. Molekk and the man on his right both sat forward in their seats, a hungry look in their eyes.

"Try again," Riard said calmly. "You'll get it soon enough."

"*Ikte…*wait, what happens when I do get it?"

"See!" Molekk looked around triumphantly. "She doesn't want to do it. She's a spy."

"I'm not allowed to tell you," Riard said. "Just say it." He lowered his tone. "Hurry up, Molekk is starting to annoy me." He winked.

"Umm …" Eiryenne didn't know which tongue she was trying to speak in or what kind of spell it was supposed to bring down on her head. But if they used it to weed out spies, it couldn't be anything pleasant. She gritted her teeth. "*Ichstemeay ralisteo damerola.*"

Nothing happened.

Molekk leaned back with a sigh of disbelief.

Riard had her repeat another few lines and then turned back to the Council. "Satisfied?"

The head councillor sighed again and gave them a curt nod. Without another word, Riard ushered Eiryenne out the door.

"What was that all about?" she asked once they'd caught up with Danzi.

"That was Yunian, the language of the unicorns," said Riard. "You can't lie in Yunian, so we use it to check for spies."

"So what did I say? *I am not a spy?*"

"Something along those lines."

Riard led her and Danzi through the camp to a low, circular hut near the meadows.

Once inside, he closed the door. Eiryenne saw green light flickering around the door frame and realized that Riard was, in fact, a mage—human or otherwise—it was hard to tell. He looked to be around forty, with dark green eyes and dimpled cheeks. There was sawdust in his curly brown beard and unkempt hair, as well as smudges of paint and soot on his robes.

He took a seat across from her and Danzi in a low-backed wooden chair and sighed. Then he chuckled. "Danzi Daggoras, returning to camp." He shook his head in disbelief. "Times sure have changed."

"Have they ever," Danzi replied quietly.

"I'm guessing that the girl was only part of the reason you've come back?"

"Obviously." Danzi took the engraved stone key from his pockets, along with a few scrolls, several amulets, and a curiously shaped bit of coral inlaid with glowing crystals.

Riard whistled. "You've been busy."

"I'm not exactly one to sit idle." Danzi took the coral, and it transformed into a glowing sword, its blade crystal, and its handle white coral. A single crack extended through the blade. "Got this in Rituff. Varcroft had four. He was going to use them to summon the Sorjets and wipe out the west coast, but I got to this one first and broke the connection." He put the sword back on the table, and it turned back into a piece of coral. "It is of no use to a lone warrior, but for an army …

you might find it useful if you can convince the Council that it's a good idea. Speaking of which," he pointed to the purple silver brooch on Riard's chest, "promotion? Senior councillor now, are we?"

"Yes. Though I'm not sure I can convince them that *you* are a good idea."

Danzi chuckled. "What more can they do to me?" He opened one of the scrolls and handed it to Riard. "I think that is self-explanatory."

Riard looked at the paper and paled. "Do I want to know where you got this?"

"No."

"Thought so."

As they continued to speak, Eiryenne noticed that there were some tapestries in this cabin as well. She recognized the same tan-armoured woman from the Council's room. But looking closer, she saw that this tapestry was faded and unkempt. A layer of dust had settled on it. On the other wall, by the window, was a tapestry of the golden winged lion. He was depicted on a blue and red patterned background, with yellow embroidery at the corners. Its edges had frayed with time, but the lion's fur gleamed without a speck of dust.

By the oval-shaped window hung a painted sheet of canvas showing a forest. Wide, green leaves crowned mossy branches, and a stream wound between the trunks, forming little pools around their roots. Lush, long grass grew along its banks, interspersed with flowers and smaller plants. The artist's signature was in the corner, though she could only make out part of it: *Ershke.*

Eiryenne returned her attention to the conversation for long enough to notice that Danzi and Riard weren't speaking Common anymore. It was a strange-sounding language, smoother than Draconic but less elegant than Yunian. They seemed to be talking about that weird stone key with the brass symbols; Riard was holding it in one hand and gesturing at it excitedly.

The girl looked back at the walls. Next to the lion tapestry was a set of shelves filled with scrolls. And in the corner, there was a large, heavy oak staff with an emerald set at its end. Eiryenne reached toward it with her mind and could feel the gem sparking with Riard's magic. There was also the hilt of a short sword poking out from beneath a pile of scrolls, but it was covered with dust.

There was a knock at the door. Riard gestured to it, and it flew open.

Standing there was a young elf around Eiryenne's age, dressed in a light blue and green tunic. He had messy, honey-coloured hair that curled lightly over his pointed ears in wild tufts. His face quivered with ill-contained excitement.

"Fosto sent me to tell you that he wants the manuscript now," he said to Riard. Then he looked at Eiryenne. "And … you have a visitor." He shot Danzi a furtive glance, then made an awkward bow and hurried out.

Eiryenne stood up, puzzled. Visitor?

2 ~ Settling In

Eiryenne wasn't sure what to expect as she waded through a sea of hostile faces. Then, close to what seemed to be the main gate, she spotted a middle-aged woman with a light brown ponytail and a wide-brimmed hat standing by a tall dun horse.

"Tina!"

"Hello!" The shepherd grinned, giving Eiryenne a hug. "It's good to see you again. I've heard all sorts of things about that quest of yours. It's a miracle you're still in one piece."

"I know." Eiryenne laughed. "We definitely had a few close calls, but it all worked out in the end."

"You'll have to tell me all about it at the campfire tonight," said Tina. "I'm sure it's quite the story." She paused and looked her over. "You look … different. More confident. Happier."

"Well, I'm sure anyone would be happy to get Tairung's necklace off them," Eiryenne said. "What about you? What are you doing here?"

"I broke away from the soldiers that attacked us, but you and Danzi were already gone. So, I went on to Rosfiord. But my quiet little hometown was quiet no longer." She sighed. "Soldiers and bandits run amok. Raids happen at least once a week. I thought about trying to find somewhere else to stay, but in the end, I decided that I'd gotten tired of running. I wanted to confront this problem at its source. So, I made my way here."

Behind her, Lahu nickered. Eiryenne went over to pet the dun stallion, feeling a pang as he stirred up memories of Neil.

The rest of the camp's inhabitants were holding back, but Riard walked up to them and shook the shepherd's hand. "Hello, Tina. It's been a while."

"Indeed. But somehow, it's still good to be back."

The mage turned to Eiryenne. "Now, Danzi says that he's taught you some basic spells and sword work. We'll have to test that out, see which of my classes you can join."

"Do it now," called out one of the teenage mages that had clustered around the gate.

"Yeah, let's see what the dragon girl's got," said another.

"Why not?" Riard shrugged. "Let's see." The youths quieted as he looked through their ranks, sizing them up. "Leo, come spar with Eiryenne."

"Sure!" The enthusiastic blonde elf who'd delivered the message to Riard's door bounded forward, grinning nervously.

Riard set Eiryenne at one end of the clearing between the tents and Leo at the other. People were trickling in at the edges, looking on curiously. Eiryenne spotted a few councillors as well as the rest of the elven youths and the girls who'd watched her arrive. Also among the onlookers were Tina, giving her a thumbs-up, and Danzi, watching silently.

Eiryenne clenched her sweaty palms. She had to do her mentor proud.

"Get ready," said Riard. "And on my signal, cast your spell. Three, two, one!"

Eiryenne reached for her magic, folding her consciousness around it like a glove. Then she raised her hand and whipped it outward, filling her spell with weight as if she were throwing a Firedrake at Leo.

"*Harutova rapt* — oooff!" The elf's incantation was cut off as a ball of Eiryenne's magic slammed him in the chest and knocked him backward. He fell onto his rear, looking surprised. But he recovered just as quickly. "Nice one. How'd you do it that fast?"

Eiryenne heard murmurs from the crowd. Tina beamed; Danzi looked satisfied.

She let out the breath she'd been holding.

"I didn't hear your incantation," Riard said.

"I didn't use one," Eiryenne said.

"Hmm." The mage looked thoughtful. "Danzi's been schooling you in instinct-based magic, hasn't he?"

The girl nodded.

"I see." Riard turned to the boy that she'd just knocked down. "Leo, give her a tour of the camp." He then addressed one of the departing onlookers; the crowd had begun to disperse upon seeing that the fight was over. "Kevrina, have a bunk and change of clothes ready."

The girl he was talking to rolled her eyes. "Fine."

Leo came up to Eiryenne. "Come on," he said. "There's lots to see."

He led her down the row of tents and buildings, rattling off names and features.

First, he pointed to a set of intricately built wooden cabins with leaves and patterns engraved on their circular walls. "Over on the left we have some of the elf cabins." They spotted some of the elf youths from before milling about them. Leo pointed out the two sentries that had greeted Eiryenne and Danzi upon arrival. "That's Tukse and

Minov. I think you've met them already." The two sentries were watching them as they passed, speaking with some of the other older elven youths. Tukse, the silver-haired one, wore a dark expression. Leo then pointed to a few boys that looked closer to his age and waved. One of them waved back. "Those are Roben and Nur. They're my friends. We'll talk to them later at archery practice."

Eiryenne walked beside him, still a little overwhelmed and trying to remember all the names.

"Then the humans' camp over there." The human cabins were simple shacks, built for convenience rather than comfort. "And the minotaurs live in those rocky things."

One thing was obvious—this camp was half-empty. There were far more buildings than people, and the majority of those they saw were kids or teenagers. The rest, Eiryenne reasoned, had to be off battling Varcroft.

There was a shout from behind them. Eiryenne turned to see the elf woman who'd tried to shoot Danzi, along with another elf, an adult male in purple and white robes. His brow was furrowed, and he was shouting at Leo in another language.

The elf boy looked sheepish. He replied in the same dialect, and Eiryenne heard Riard's name. Then Leo turned and led her in the opposite direction.

"Your parents?" she asked.

He shook his head. "Aunt and uncle. My father wouldn't have minded this."

They had just rounded a patch of minotaur abodes when the sound of different voices speaking Common reached their ears.

"… the way she *dresses*, honestly."

"And that filth! … hair is awful …"

"What an ugly broad …"

"… honestly expect her to bunk with *us*?"

They walked right into a gaggle of girls clustered around the door to a cabin. Each of them jumped then glared at Eiryenne with their noses turned up as if she were the most repulsive thing they had ever seen. Looking at them, all wearing fancy cotton dresses and with hair more spotless than Riard's tapestry, Eiryenne suddenly became very aware that her torn-up clothes were caked with dried mud and blood, and twigs were tangled in her dirty hair. She hadn't washed since Balon's castle, and her dishevelled appearance never seemed more out of place.

Eiryenne blinked. Since when did that matter?

"E r..." Leo hastened his step as they walked past them. The girls turned and whispered to each other behind their hands, pointing discreetly at them and giggling as though sharing a secret joke.

Eiryenne rubbed her forehead. She didn't see what was so funny. But seeing these girls was an uncomfortable reminder of her former village life and the way that the other kids had bullied her.

"Right." Leo stopped at the south end of the camp, where meadows dotted with horses bordered the forests. He pointed out the archery range, a field with wooden targets. A little way from it was an open arena with walls made of trees: the combat arena. The forest beyond it was also part of the camp, used in training exercises and for hunting.

"And those are the stables," he finished, gesturing to a set of stalls set beneath a leafy roof by the fenced pastures. "That's where I work. Everyone's got chores around camp; mine are looking after the horses and other animals."

"Other animals?" Eiryenne looked closer at the larger paddocks behind the arena. There was something moving inside them, but from this distance she couldn't see what it was.

"Yeah. You'll see."

They paused at the edge of the empty barracks, across from a hill covered with grazing horses. Eiryenne looked at them longingly. They were beautiful: rich bays, golden palominos, and striking chestnuts. One pasture contained the tall, muscular animals she knew had to be warhorses. Of these there were only a handful. Another field had horses that were lightly built and fleet of foot. In the last two were mixtures of different horses, ponies, and mules.

"So ..." Leo's tone had changed. He tried to sound casual, but his voice was charged with a combination of nerves and excitement. "What's he like?"

"Huh?" Eiryenne tore her gaze from the horses. "Who?"

"*Danzi.*"

"What about him?"

"What do you mean, *what about him*?" Leo gasped. "He's a living legend. And you got to spend *weeks* with him." He sounded both impressed and jealous. "Tell me! Haven't you seen him in action?"

"Well, " Eiryenne shrugged, "yes, I've seen him fight. He's really good with that longsword. And he shoots fire at people."

"Details, please," Leo implored. There was a faraway look in his eyes. "Everyone knows Danzi shoots fire at people. But you can tell me what it's like to stand there and watch him battle."

"Okay, well, there was this one time we came across some bandits …" Eiryenne began. "And he leaped and whirled and hacked with his blade, and no one could so much as touch him." She recounted the battle in as much detail as she could remember.

"What about spells?" the elf asked eagerly. "Has he done any really crazy ones?"

"Um, let's see …" Eiryenne thought back to their journey. She described the torrents of fire that rolled off Danzi's scales and the infernos that he'd send to engulf his enemies, as well as the fiery tornado from the final battle against the ice creature.

Leo drank in every detail with wide eyes. The whole scene reminded her of how Hayden used to tell her his stories.

"That is amazing. I wish *I* could do that." The elf grinned. "Would be pretty great, wouldn't it? To be the master of fire?"

"I guess," she said. "But it looks like it's hard to control. Think of all the things you'd burn by accident. Best to leave fire to the dragons."

But Leo was already moving on to his next question. "What kind of things did you do? Was the Necklace hard to carry? And are people in the Empire still scared of him?"

Eiryenne narrowed her eyes. "Why are you so interested in this all of a sudden?" It occurred to her that details of Danzi's skills and deeds might be of interest to people besides the common passerby. And it was obvious that he had enemies in camp.

Leo hesitated. "Er, well … everyone else in camp hates him. Everyone except Riard. They're scared. They mention things he's done before. Bad things." Eiryenne frowned.

"Um, I'm not supposed to talk about it, sorry." Leo did look genuinely disappointed. "Come on, I think they've got your bunk ready by now."

He led her back to the human cabins and pointed to one at the left of the group. It was covered with peeling paint that had once been purple. One window was stained pink.

Leo departed as soon as he'd shown her the cabin, so Eiryenne opened the door herself and walked in.

On the inside, the cabin was slightly more ornate. Though the wood was roughly hewn, several sheets of embroidered silk hung on it. There were eight bunk beds, four per wall. The girls that Eiryenne had spotted before were lounging on them, tittering. One of the older girls, a brunette with her hair tied on top of her head in a strange knot, gave the girl in front of her a push. Head low, the second girl approached Eiryenne with hesitant steps.

"Here," she said, gingerly holding out a bundle of clothes.

Eiryenne took the clothes and examined them: a simple brown shirt with a leather collar and a crinkled green skirt. She'd had worse. "Thanks. What's your name?"

"Water's out the back," interrupted one of the other girls. "Scrub off that stench before you talk to us. We're dying here." She pretended to choke and gag. The others did the same.

Eiryenne shrugged and turned back out the door. People could be weird sometimes.

At the back of the cabin, she found another door leading to a small room with a washbasin and a shallow tub. Not as luxurious as Balon's castle, but it would have to do. Once she'd cleaned up, changed, and scrubbed her old clothes, she slung what was left of her pack over her shoulder and headed back into the main cabin to confront the girls.

"Your bunk's over there," said the girl who'd given her the clothes. "And my name's Taymel." She looked to be about Eiryenne's age, with olive skin and black hair.

Eiryenne walked over to the bunk and put her few possessions onto it. There wasn't much left of her pack, but her sword and dagger were still in working order. She put them beside the pack, suddenly unsure about leaving them there.

Something brushed her wrist. "So, you're the dragon girl," said a deeper voice behind her.

Eiryenne straightened and turned. The speaker was a stocky girl with long, jet-black hair and pale skin. She was wearing a purple shirt and white skirt. Her eyes glittered with something between dread and curiosity.

"I travelled with the dragon, yes."

"Anyway, what's your name?" asked Taymel.

"Eiryenne," she replied. "It's nice to meet you all."

"Of course," said the girl in purple and white in a very dry tone. "I'm Hilla."

"Cassandra," said the teen on her right. Her light blonde hair spilled over her shoulders and pooled in the cuffs and laces in her maroon tunic. "So, what's the—"

"Hello. Introductions," interrupted the girl behind her, the one who'd pushed Taymel to give Eiryenne the clothes. She had a shrill, high-pitched voice and wide blue eyes. Some sort of strange dark substance was smeared around them. "My name's Mels, and that's Kevrina up there."

Kevrina sat casually on the top bunk at the left corner of the room. Hers was the window-stained pink, which matched her dress and necklace. She looked coldly down at the newcomer.

Eiryenne touched her wrist, realizing that the glass bead with her name on it was missing, in addition to Danzi's warming amulet. "Hey, who took my—" She saw something sparkling in Hilla's hands and tried to take a big step toward her. But it had been months since she'd worn a skirt, and the garment caught around her legs. Tripping, Eiryenne fell flat on her face.

Laughter echoed around the room.

"Too used to flying? Forgotten how to walk, have you?" giggled Cassandra.

Kevrina slid down from her bunk as Eiryenne struggled to her feet. "Now, what have we here?" She took the bracelets from Hilla and held up the glass bead first. "Garbage." She tossed it back to Hilla. "Now, this ..." The amulet glittered gold and red in her hands.

Eiryenne's face was red. The insides of her skirt had turned slippery, twisting, and turning around her thrashing legs until they were bound together. "Give it back."

"Or what?" Kevrina laughed and slid the amulet's chain around her own wrist.

Eiryenne grimaced. She was having trouble accessing her magic for some reason. Every time she reached for it, it felt drawn down to her tangled-up ankles and refused to cooperate.

"Come on," said Mels. "Supper'll be ready soon. Let's go."

Still laughing, the other girls followed her out of the room.

"What did I do?" muttered Eiryenne. "I just met you."

Taymel lingered behind. She crouched beside the other girl. "Initiation rite," she said. "Ever heard of it?"

She frowned. "What?"

"Y'know," Taymel fiddled with the hem of her shirt, "give the new girl a hard time, see what she's made of. Just forget it. You'll be a part of the gang in no time." It didn't sound like she believed what she was saying. Then, giving Eiryenne a hesitant look, she hurried out of the cabin.

Eiryenne took a couple of deep breaths. "Calm down," she muttered. "You're not in mortal danger. Just a couple of silly girls playing pranks on you." Now that they were out of the room, she found that she could concentrate better. She turned her attention to the skirt that was tangling her legs. There was a strange kind of magic in the fabric, something that pulled and sucked her flesh and magic alike. Running a mental finger along it, Eiryenne mulled it over until she found a point where it had unravelled slightly. Grabbing hold of it, she unravelled it further, sliding her own spells underneath the enchantment until she could ease it out of the fabric. It took her longer than she would have liked, as her own magic often got stuck along the way.

She was red-faced and frustrated with herself by the time she was done. She'd faced all kinds of monsters on the road, and yet here she was having trouble with a bunch of human girls.

Slowly, she got up and slid the skirt off. Kevrina must have asked one of the elves to enchant it. If everyone got that treatment when they arrived here, she couldn't see how they managed to enjoy the stay.

Eiryenne turned to her bunk. Her sword and dagger were gone. But no one had touched her old, soggy clothes. Her breeches still smelled, but at least they were almost dry and decidedly magic-free. She put them on and walked out.

At first, she had no intention of trying to find wherever supper was, but her stomach soon dictated otherwise, and she followed the smell of food until she came to a large tent set up near the middle of the camp, the front flap pegged wide open. Tables lined with meat, bread, vegetables, and other foods she couldn't identify stood in a row beneath it, with a line-up of campers before them. Each person or creature took a plate from a nearby bench and then walked along the tables, scooping up food as they went. Eiryenne watched them until she got the idea of how it worked. Then she waited until the crowd cleared before taking a plate herself. She scooped up a bit of everything, apart from the raw meat and organs at the end of the aisle. Then she followed the others to a clearing outside the tent filled with low wooden tables and benches. Groups of humans, elves, mages, minotaurs, and shapeshifters sat there, eating, and talking.

The talking quietened as she stepped from the shadows of the tent.

Kevrina and Hilla were sitting with the rest of the girls and a couple of boys— three were human, the other was an elf. Looking at him, Eiryenne recognized Tukse, the sentry. It must have been him who enchanted her skirt.

They had all been examining the shiny amulet on Kevrina's wrist but fell silent as they saw Eiryenne. Hilla pinched Cassandra's shoulder. "You owe me five cronos ..." she whispered.

Eiryenne looked away, scanning the tables for somewhere to sit. Having so many pairs of eyes on her was unnerving, but there was no familiar face to park herself beside.

".. couldn't have done it that fast."

"... knew she was a freak."

She tried to concentrate on the sound of the tent's corner flapping in the wind, but the whispers drilled into her head as if they were shouting at her. Everywhere she turned, there were people muttering, looking over their shoulders with suspicion. There was hate in those eyes. Fear, too. They were looking at her the same way they'd looked at Danzi. But he was nowhere to be seen.

Then more voices reached her ears. They were coming from behind.

"Gonna make a laughingstock of us, you are."

"Don't do it, man, you know Uncle said to keep away from her."

"Come on, Leo, let it go."

Eiryenne turned her head just enough to see who was talking. Leo was standing next to two other elf boys — his friends Roben and Nur. They looked like they were trying to talk him out of something. Roben had a hand on his shoulder. Leo shrugged it off.

Over at their table, the girls continued to laugh and joke. Eiryenne wished she could sink into the ground or invent a spell that would invisibly plug her ears.

"Annoying, aren't they?" Leo had walked over to her. "They drive me crazy, too, sometimes. Come on, let's go sit over there." He led her over to one of the tables in the back.

The only other occupant of the table was a teenage boy with a chubby face and enormous torso. He had short dark hair that stuck straight up and coal black eyes with a friendly gleam. His plate was stacked with food up to his chin, and his stomach bulged through his grubby shirt.

"Hi, Grindt," Leo said with a tight smile, sitting down. "Hope you don't mind."

"Of course not." Grindt gave them a broad grin. "How's it going, Leo? Who's your friend? Newcomer, right?"

"Hello," Eiryenne said politely. "I'm Eiryenne."

"Nice name," Grindt said. Eiryenne searched his bulging face for traces of sarcasm or scorn but found none. "How do you like camp?"

"It's different than what I expected," she said truthfully.

As they sat down, Roben came over and grabbed Leo's arm. "What are you doing?" he hissed. Either he thought that humans had ears made of lead, or he didn't care that he was overheard. "You're sitting at the losers' table."

"Today it's the winners' table," Eiryenne told him. "You're welcome to join us."

The elf stared at her. Then he backed off and walked to another table with Nur.

"Well," Leo said. He turned back to Eiryenne. "And on that cheerful note—"

She realized he probably had more questions about Danzi. "Look," she began. "I know you probably want to hear more about my travels, but I hope you don't mind if I eat first. The last thing I ate was a piece of half-cooked spotted deer that Danzi killed this morning. I'm hungry, and I don't know what this is, but it smells delicious."

Grindt nodded. "That's the spirit," he said. "Always need to fuel up before you can get down to business."

Leo looked like he was going to say something but changed his mind and turned to his plate.

Eiryenne dug in. She inhaled masses of strange meat and sliced vegetables, topping her meal off with sweetened bread and a cup of fresh apple cider. Just like the camp, the tables were obviously built for more people than were present. The other teens and kids sat at a large cluster of wooden tables, but they only occupied a fraction of them. Eiryenne looked over Grindt's shoulder at the tables on the far side of the tent. She saw some of the adults there, as well as a handful of Council members. Their tables were wrought with iron.

A shadow fell over Eiryenne's table. She looked up to see a raven-haired man dressed in a sky-blue tunic and navy-blue vest. Two long daggers hung at his waist. He looked vaguely familiar, but with all the new faces she'd seen that day, for a second Eiryenne had a bit of trouble figuring out where she'd seen him before.

"Ah, so it's true," he said in a smooth, light voice. He had a short, neat black beard and blue eyes. Looking closer, Eiryenne saw familiar slitted pupils.

Danzi's brother.

"Lianos?" she said.

He smiled. "It's good to see you here, Eiryenne. I had my doubts, but that's the thing about Danzi. He never stops surprising you."

Silence fell over a better portion of the tables. Leo choked on his food.

Eiryenne and Lianos both turned to see Danzi standing in the shadow between two cabins next to the meal hall. He was still wearing the same bloodstained and muddy clothes Eiryenne had last seen him in. Without another word, Lianos strode over to him, and the two engaged in a rapid conversation in Draconic.

Leo took a sip of his cider. "You know Lianos?"

Eiryenne shrugged. "We've met."

"Makes sense. I heard that he was off on some dangerous mission deep into the Empire. He must've just gotten back." Leo sighed. "They get to do all the fun stuff while we're stuck over here."

"I *like* being stuck over here," Grindt said. "You know why? Because I like staying *alive*."

"Now." Leo clapped his hands eagerly and turned to Eiryenne. "You were saying something about giving us a summary of your epic adventures."

"Hang on," Grindt said. "Something's happening."

Indeed, there were shouts coming from the councillors' table.

"Lianos," thundered the head councillor. "Get over here."

The dragon mage looked up from where he was talking with Danzi. There was a frown on his face. Danzi leaned forward and muttered something in his ear, then wandered off toward the meal hall. Lianos sighed and strode over to Councillor Molekk.

"Yes, Councillor?" he said.

"You should know," Molekk began. "That this council sentenced Danzi Daggoras to death several hours ago."

"And lot of progress they've made on that front," Eiryenne muttered. Leo snorted into his drink.

Lianos didn't look surprised. His expression mild, he stood with his hands clasped behind his back, waiting for Molekk to continue.

"We voted against doing so before Hurraine's return because we didn't have the magepower to contain him," continued Molekk. "But we do now."

Lianos raised his eyebrows. "Sir?"

"Kill him."

3 ~ Clash of Fire

Lianos looked taken aback. He glanced from Molekk to Danzi, who had sauntered out of the meal tent and was standing by the neighbouring table.

Around them, people were edging out of their seats.

"You heard me," Molekk repeated. "Kill him!"

Danzi gave his brother a look and said something in Draconic. Lianos's jaw tightened as he gazed into the other mage's fiery eyes. Then he looked at the ground, hesitating.

"Kill him, soldier," the councillor to Molekk's right shouted. "That's an *order*."

Lianos looked torn. He half-heartedly ran a hand along the hilt of one of his daggers, glancing again between his brother and the councillor. The tension in the air between the three of them was palpable.

"Oh, this is interesting," Leo leaned forward, whispering in Eiryenne's ear. "Lianos *always* follows orders."

"He's not really gonna kill him, is he?" she murmured. She studied the doubt in Lianos's eyes. There was something else, too. Was it fear?

Danzi was speaking in Draconic again. *"You knew this day would come, Lianos. So, little brother, what's it going to be?"*

"What are they saying?" demanded Molekk.

Across from him, Riard shrugged. "I don't know. It's Draconic."

"Who here speaks it?" the councillor asked.

"Just the dragons. That's kind of the point," Riard replied.

Lianos took a deep breath. "With all due respect, Councillor," he said, switching back to Common. "I don't think that's a good idea."

"What do you mean?" Molekk burst out. "I know you can do it!"

The fire mages exchanged more words in Draconic.

"What do you think they're saying?" whispered Leo.

"Shh," Eiryenne said. She was watching the exchange with rapt attention, and even though she didn't understand a word, she didn't want to miss a second.

Suddenly, the brothers fell silent.

As if on cue, both of them released a wave of fire. Orange and blue flames clashed in the middle and exploded, setting half the tables aflame.

Eiryenne followed the crowd as they ran from the smoke and heat, sprinting between the tents until they reached a small field free of buildings. There they all paused, catching their breath, and peering out over the tents, trying to see the battle.

Two shapes hurtled over the tops of the cabins in front of them, landing with a thud in the middle of the clearing in another splash of flames. Councillors, warriors, and teenagers alike all stumbled back, leaving a space in the middle where the two figures faced off.

Eiryenne lost track of Grindt in the confusion, but Leo was crouched next to her, his hands over his mouth and his eyes wide. As the smoke cleared, they could see Lianos and Danzi facing off. In a flash, Danzi drew his broadsword and Lianos unsheathed his long, slightly curved knives. They charged at one another, almost faster than the eye could follow. Danzi swung his sword overhead as Eiryenne had seen so many times before. She half-expected it to cleave Lianos in half. But the other fire mage raised his hands almost too quickly for her eye to follow, and with a thundering clash of metal on metal, Danzi's sword landed squarely on Lianos's crossed blades. The metal of their weapons creaked and bent, as though protesting the sheer amount of force that they were being subjected to.

Danzi had clearly put all his strength behind the swing, and he continued to put pressure on the blade, trying to force it downward. But though Lianos's arms shook with effort, his blades did not yield, and he held Danzi at bay.

Then Lianos parried the blade with his left knife and drove the right one toward Danzi's ribs. Danzi wrenched his sword free and blocked the blow, then swung his blade in a ferocious diagonal cut. Lianos ducked and jumped out of the way. He recovered his footing just as Danzi charged him, and their flashing blades clashed once more in a shower of sparks.

Danzi was fast, but Lianos matched his speed. His blades moved around his hands so quickly that he seemed to be holding twin snakes of liquid metal that flowed around his fists and never held still for more than a second. Eiryenne wasn't actually sure whether to call them very long daggers or rather short swords; but each of them was at least a foot shorter than Danzi's sword and a lot thinner.

The two dragon mages leaped high into the air, their hands a blur, exchanging blows with inhuman speed and strength. Lianos was the first to land. He rolled out of the way of Danzi's first strike then jumped over his sword and sent his dagger snaking toward his neck. Danzi ducked beneath it, raising his sword, and blocking the second dagger with the flat of his blade. As they continued to fight, the fire mages' deadly blades came within inches of one another, but somehow, they always found the space to block or the time to dodge.

The raven-haired mage's movements were fluid as he dodged and danced around his brother's sweeping attacks. He leaned back and pivoted at an impossible angle to avoid Danzi's slashing sword, then slammed one of his knives against the hilt, almost knocking it out of his hands. But Danzi recovered quickly, and he brought his sword up to Lianos's neck just as he thrust his remaining dagger at Danzi's gut.

They froze. Lianos looked at the crowd and met Molekk's gaze. He tapped the blade that rested against his jugular. "Decapitation," he then gestured to his own dagger, which was pressed against Danzi's belly, "versus incapacitation. You'd lose your only other dragon, and he'd still be alive. Wounded, for sure, but no guarantees there. And a burned-up camp to boot. You still think it's worth it?"

Molekk opened and closed his mouth wordlessly.

"I think he got the point," Danzi said. The dragon mages both stood back and sheathed their weapons.

"They *planned* all that?" Leo muttered as he and Eiryenne made their way back to what was left of the tables. One of the camp mages had put out most of the fires, but many of the tables and surrounding buildings were reduced to smouldering ruins.

"They must've. If they were really trying to kill each other, I think there'd be a lot more carnage," she replied. "The councillors weren't listening to why having Lianos fight Danzi was a bad idea so they decided to show them."

"Guys!" Grindt had caught up with them. "Look, our table survived. Who wants seconds?"

"Nah, I'm good," the elf said. They took a seat. "But grab me another cup of cider, will you?"

Grindt waddled off to the food tent, which was miraculously still standing.

"Now that was some extreme sword fighting," Leo said. "And the look on Molekk's face when the tables all blew up. Priceless."

The light was starting to dim as evening draped over the sky. Leo explained that there was some kind of magical lighting system that usually kicked in after dark, but apparently the dragons' sparring match had taken that out, too, so the teens kept several of the broken tables and benches alight, giving a ruddy glow to their faces. When Danzi strode by, the impromptu campfire in front of them blazed several feet higher and gave off a shower of sparks.

Shortly after Grindt returned from the food tent, another figure approached their table, plate in hand.

"Well, I knew I'd be late for supper," Tina said as she came up to them. "But it seems I missed a whole lot more than that." She took a seat next to them. "The Council will have fun cleaning up this mess, I'm sure." Then the shepherd glanced at the boys. "I see you're making friends already, Eiryenne."

After Leo and Grindt introduced themselves, Tina leaned close to Eiryenne and whispered in her ear. "We're pretty close to the fire, and you didn't even flinch when Danzi walked by and made it bigger."

"No, fire's not a problem anymore," she replied quietly. "Danzi took care of that."

Tina squeezed her arm. "I'm proud of you." Then she leaned back and spoke in a normal tone again. "So! You've been doing quite a lot of travelling since I last saw you. You promised me a story, and by the looks of things this elf here is dying to hear what you've got to say."

Eiryenne laughed and looked around at their eager faces. "All right." She began telling them about her journey with Danzi. She described their trek through the Empire and the creatures they had faced. Though she glanced over the parts that had to do with her own personal terrors, she left out few details of the battles and Tairung's destructive power. She also didn't mention Danzi's crystal cave or his unicorn horn, honouring his wishes. While she spoke, she could see out of the corner of her eye that some of the other teens were listening in, but she found that she didn't care.

A couple of times, Leo looked like he was going to interrupt, but Tina shushed him and gestured for Eiryenne to continue. When she came to the final battle between Danzi and the ice mage, however, he couldn't contain himself.

"Wait, so the ground opened up?" he exclaimed. "How long was the ice mage in there? And he *bit through* an oberon? Their skin's supposed to be thicker than anything! And you actually shot an ogre ... twice?"

"Leo, let her finish," Tina said.

Eiryenne managed to get through the final confrontation with the Firedrake without any more interruptions. She felt her audience draw their breath and tense as she described the last exchange of blows, then let it out as she told them how the Necklace and Firedrake both turned to dust.

"Wow, that is amazing," Leo burst out. "I can't believe you got to do all that. You're so lucky."

"*Lucky?* Look how many times she almost died," Grindt retorted. "I think she's lucky to be alive."

Tina nodded. "It sounded like an unpredictable, harrowing journey, and I congratulate you on getting through it successfully." She raised her glass in a toast, and the others did the same.

Eiryenne watched Tukse as she walked back to the cabin. He split off from the girls well before they reached it. Perhaps that meant they were done with the magical pranks, for today at least.

Indeed, her bunk was free of magic when she reached it. After sleeping on the ground for months, it felt luxuriously soft. Despite wanting to stay awake for a little while to keep an eye on the girls, Eiryenne's eyelids soon began to droop. She was fast asleep before all of them had even gotten back to the cabin.

Eiryenne knew she was in trouble even before she opened her eyes. She felt hot and sticky all over. The girl tried to get up, but her hair was stuck to the pillow, and every motion caused a painful pricking in her scalp.

Gingerly, she turned her head to look around the room. By the looks of things, it was still early. There was barely any light coming in from under the closed window, and all the other girls were fast asleep, snoring in their bunks. There was a mirror against the wall opposite Eiryenne, strategically placed so that she could see her own reflection.

Pink and purple paint was smeared across her entire body. It glued her hair to the pillow in wild spikes and stuck her clothes to the bedsheets. There was red paint splashed across her lips and bands of black drawn on her face.

Eiryenne blinked. She must have been sleeping deeply for them to have done all that. Her suspicions were confirmed when she spotted a sweet-smelling leaf on her pillow. Even sniffing it made her feel drowsy—it must have been a sleeping herb like the ones Danzi had once pointed out. She got up slowly, not wanting to wake up any of the others. She could do without their laughter right now. The pillow and bedsheets remained stuck to her clothes and hair. She dragged them out the door after her and walked over to the room with the water basin. But when she splashed the liquid over her skin, it burned. Eiryenne stumbled back with a yelp and spilled the water all over her arms.

Angry welts sprang up over her skin, multiplying until they turned into masses of boils.

Eiryenne ground her teeth in embarrassed indignation. She opened the door with swollen fingers. What was she going to do now?

First things first. She had to find a basin with proper water in it, not that strange liquid the girls had poured into theirs. A horse trough would do, if only the stables weren't on the other side of camp, she thought.

As she stepped out onto the path, Eiryenne hoped that it would be too early for anyone to be out and about. The thought of being seen in this state made her cringe.

The skin around her eyes started to swell, obscuring her vision. She ended up walking right into a wall. But unfortunately, her ears remained clear enough to hear the peals of laughter that greeted her. Squinting, she could make out several shapes near the elf cabins. One of them was Tukse, laughing so hard that he held his belly.

Evidently, she was not the only one that got up before dawn around here.

Eiryenne's cheeks turned red and burned as she continued to stumble around blindly. Her resolve to find the stables dimmed by the second, replaced by desperation and the beginnings of panic. For the umpteenth time, she wished she knew an invisibility spell.

Bonk. Her forehead hit something hard and wooden that had missed her outstretched arms. She shook her head and kept going.

After two more walls she ran into something softer.

"Wha—?" Whoever she'd walked into turned around, sounding surprised. "Don't tell me that's a new fashion."

Eiryenne recognized the voice. Lianos. "Umm … not exactly. My cabin mates decided to prank me again."

She heard the dragon mage sigh. "Kids." He shook his head then peered into her face. "Hmm, looks like a combination of harrow root paint combined with tark potion and—"

"Can you get it off?" Eiryenne tried to keep her voice steady.

"Follow me." To avoid getting the potion on his skin, Lianos turned his hand into a dragon paw before grabbing her sleeve. He led her through the rows of tents and cabins that were reduced to blurry shapes in Eiryenne's puffed-up eyes. Then they stepped into a building, and though she couldn't see it, Eiryenne could sense Riard's magic.

"Oh, dear," he said when he saw them. "Rough morning?"

"You could say that," she mumbled.

She heard Riard get up and fiddle with some glass bottles. Then there was a spark of green magic, and the liquid lit up briefly.

"Here you go." He poured the potion over her head. It gave off a gentle cooling sensation, quickly soothing her burning skin. Within seconds, the boils shrank down and disappeared.

Eiryenne sighed with relief. "Thank you." She was still coloured pink, but the welts were gone, and she could see again.

"That'll wash off now," Riard said. "There's a water trough out back and to the left. Just drain it when you're done." He turned to Lianos and chuckled. "I've seen a lot of red on those claws, but never pink."

The dragon mage smiled slightly. "I know." He raised his hand, which was still a dragon paw but with splotches of pink paint where he'd grabbed the girl's sleeve. A small tongue of blue fire appeared, running along his claws until it had burned off all the paint. Eiryenne caught a glimpse of sapphire-blue scales before his paw morphed back into a hand. More fire sprang up on his vest to burn off the paint that had evidently gotten there when Eiryenne bumped into him.

After she washed off the rest of the paint and untangled her hair, Eiryenne walked slowly through the camp, her clothes still dripping wet. She had no intention of going back to her cabin. Who knew what other nasty surprises were in store for her there?

The sun had risen in earnest by now, sitting on top of the eastern horizon like a big, burning egg, setting alight the clouds that surrounded it.

Eiryenne sighed and brushed the wet hair out of her eyes. She wasn't sure what she'd expected, but it definitely hadn't been this. There was no place for her here. Kevrina and the others were making that clear.

She wandered to the southern reaches of the camp, searching for the stables. The horses, at least, would have no prejudice against her.

Eiryenne rounded a corner and stopped. She'd reached the end of the buildings, and instead of stables she saw Danzi going through his usual morning stretches in the grassy field.

She hesitated then walked up to him. "May I join you?"

He shrugged and continued the routine. Eiryenne took that as a yes and stepped into the rhythm beside him. The familiar motions started to calm her as she concentrated on them, taking her mind off Kevrina and what further torments she had in store.

Danzi's motions sped up as he transitioned from stretches to blows, and Eiryenne matched him. But as they finished the warm-up and Eiryenne turned to Danzi, expecting their usual sparring match, the dragon mage began to walk away.

Training her was not his job anymore.

Later in the morning, as Eiryenne walked into the meal hall for breakfast, she noticed Hilla pinch Cassandra again. "Ten cronos now," she whispered.

Cassandra frowned. "Drat! That's the last time I'm betting against you."

"Eat up," Leo told her as she sat down. "I heard you'll be starting weapons practice today. And magic lessons, too."

"Sounds like fun."

After breakfast, Leo led her to a large tent near the stables. On the inside it was wide and spacious. Around the perimeter the floor was covered in thick, soft rugs with big pillows to sit on, while the middle had a section of hard carpet. One side of the tent's canvas was enchanted to be transparent. Eiryenne could see the rest of the camp and the sky, with several larks passing by. Beneath the makeshift window there was a heavy oak desk covered with books, quills, and small glass vials with liquids and leaves of various colours.

Leo went to sit with Roben and Nur on the left side of the semicircle of pillows. Eiryenne sat down a few spots over. The rest of the class were mostly elves around her own age, but she spotted a few shapeshifters as well. No other humans, as expected.

Then the tent flap opened, and Riard walked in. His green robes swished around his feet as he rounded the class and took a seat on top of the oak desk, clearing a space next to a vial of something that fizzed.

He clapped his hands. "Well, good morning everyone. I'm sure you're all eager to do some more spellcasting, and believe me, we'll get to that once the senior section has arrived. They're out with Toverick at the moment. So, I thought we'd start off with a bit of theory."

Everyone around Eiryenne groaned.

"Let's start with, what is magic?"

"Magic is energy," said a boy on Eiryenne's right. He had short, thick brown hair, a straight, long nose, and big black eyes. Since he had no pointed ears, she assumed he was a shapeshifter of some kind. "It's energy that we can use and manipulate with our wills. Some people generate it naturally. We call those people mages."

"That's right, Larkden," Riard said. "Now, can someone please describe the nature of spell-casting?"

Larkden's hand shot up again.

"Know-it-all," muttered Nur. Roben stifled a laugh.

"Okay, Larkden, let's hear it," said Riard. He shot Roben a disapproving glance. "And the rest of you would do well to listen. I might quiz you on this next time."

"Well, most spells are cast using incantations," Larkden said. "We say exactly what we want the magic to do and channel the energy through our words."

"Very good. Now tell us about the difference between incantations and instinct-based magic, as well as the advantages and disadvantages of both."

"Instinct-based magic is less stable," Larkden began. "You're casting the spell with your mind, and it's really easy to think the wrong thing or lose control of what you're doing. If your thoughts aren't structured, your magic won't be. It is especially dangerous to add emotion to magic, because it will cause your spells to react in dangerous and unpredictable ways. Words are far more reliable, if slower."

"Excellent," said Riard. "Now, I want everybody to pair up and start reciting the levitation and buffering spells I had you memorize last week. Get the pronunciation right until it flows from your lips like water. Then take a leaf and make it fly." He gestured to the row of large, broad leaves that lay on his desk. With a swish of his staff, he sent them sailing toward his students.

Eiryenne looked at Leo, but he had already paired up with Roben. She turned, watching to see whether there was anyone else without a partner, but it seemed like everyone had already picked one out.

As the partners spread out in the centre of the tent and started practicing, Eiryenne spotted Larkden, still at his seat. She hesitated, then walked over to him.

"Do you have a partner?" she asked.

"No." He got up with a sigh. "But I suppose you'll do."

Just then, Riard walked over to them.

"Since you've never trained with words before, I'll give you a few tips to start off," he said, taking a seat next to her and Larkden. He took a leaf and put it in front of her. "Now, the incantation is *horali* to make the leaf levitate."

Eiryenne stared at the leaf. "*Horali.*" It didn't budge. She felt stupid. This was something she could've done so easily without the incantation.

"You're used to putting your will to the actual object. Now you have to learn to put your will to your words," Riard said. "Draw upon your magic like you always do, then let it flow through the syllables of the incantation."

She tried again, drawing upon her magic. "*Horali.*" The leaf still didn't budge.

Riard sighed. "Picture a gate. Your magic must flow through that gate to reach its destination. And once it's at that gate, your words can sculpt it into whatever you like."

Next to them, Larkden had long since tuned out their conversation. He was muttering fervently under his breath, and his leaf appeared to be tap-dancing.

Focusing, Eiryenne tried again. And again. Nothing worked.

"Keep practicing," Riard said. Then he left them to go check on the other pairs.

With no further progress, she was soon bored with the exercise. Turning, she instead started to observe the other mages at work. But to the naked eye there was not much to be seen. So, she took a few deep breaths and called upon the mage's vision that Danzi had shown her. Her view changed. Now she could see every person in the room lit up by a network of coloured light. She watched as Leo, glowing with light yellow, spoke his incantation. The magic within him seemed to pause then gather up and change shape before flowing out to the leaf in front of him and boosting it into the air.

The words were connected to the magic; it flowed through the mages' lips and was shaped by their words, spreading out according to their commands. So that, then, was what an incantation looked like from the side. She just had to figure out how to make it work for her.

Eiryenne turned her gaze to the side. She had to narrow her eyes to see Larkden's magic. It was dim and pearly grey, twitching and reshaping with his every word. The speed of his speech made it look like his magic vibrated.

Then a shadow fell over her, and she looked up to see Riard, shining with his own brand of green magic.

He looked slightly amused. "Looking for inspiration now, are we?"

Eiryenne blushed and dropped her gaze. The magical glows faded. She'd forgotten that most other mages could sense when they were being looked at.

"Just trying to figure out what it looks like," she said. "Incantations, I mean. I'm trying to see how they work." She then glanced at Larkden again, so deeply absorbed by his spells that he paid them no attention whatsoever. "His magic is strange. Is he a shapeshifter?" she asked.

Riard sat down next to her. "No. He's a Kive. They're a tribal people from the west, mostly known for their prophets and seers. You've probably met his sister, Hilla."

"They're not human?"

"Nope," Riard looked amused. "There are a lot more races out there than just humans and elves, you know. We have our fair share of them at the camp. Or rather, we did."

Eiryenne turned back to her leaf and tried her incantation again. Still no luck.

Larkden's leaf was twitching and jumping at his every word, but it never moved more than a few inches off the ground. He was rattling off words quicker than Eiryenne could make them out, while most of the others were using just a couple.

"He knows a lot of incantations."

"Larkden has a great mind," Riard said. "If he had the magic to back up all the spells he knows, we'd be in trouble." He chuckled.

Eiryenne turned back to her leaf. She pulled at her magic again, letting it trickle through her consciousness and flow through a gate that she imagined at her lips. She pictured a sculptor at the gate, waiting to carve out whatever shape she ordered out of the magic.

"*Horali.*" For a brief instant she felt a sense of connectivity between her magic and her words, and her leaf fluttered up a few inches before falling back down again.

"There we go," Riard said with a smile. He got up and walked back to his desk. Then he glanced out the window. "I'll be right back," he said. "Something's taking Toverick too long." He walked out of the tent, staff in hand.

Nur laughed. "I bet Tukse's hexed him again," he said.

Leo grinned. "Probably."

Larkden didn't notice Riard leave. He continued to mutter things to his leaf.

With a quick word in Elvish, Roben sent the leaf spiralling out of the boy's reach. "What a nerd," he sneered. "Playtime's over, didn't you hear?"

Just then the tent flap opened, and a group of older teens strode in. Eiryenne recognized Tukse at the head, along with Minov, the other sentry who'd admitted her and Danzi to the camp.

"*Reso glanca!*"

She barely had time to see who was behind them before she began to sink into the pillow she sat on. Its fabric stuck to her breeches and appeared to swallow her legs. She recognized the same magic that had enchanted her skirt. The more she fought it, the more tangled she became.

A strand of fabric detached from the pillow and slid up her torso to wrap itself around her face, squeezing it painfully tight.

"Well, well, well, what do we have here?" a voice said. Eiryenne looked around, but Tukse was sitting on the other side of the tent next to Nur and the other elves. He looked smug, but there was no sign of magic around his hands.

With some effort, Eiryenne turned her head. Kevrina and Hilla stood at the entrance. But Kevrina was the one with pinkish burgundy light shining around her hands.

"I should have known," she said. "It's no wonder you got out of my other traps so easily."

"She's like you?" Hilla asked.

"Unfortunately." Kevrina frowned distastefully.

Eiryenne didn't know what to say.

Kevrina was another human mage.

4 ~ Rivals

Eiryenne always thought that if she'd ever met another human mage, they'd be friends. And yet here she was, at the mercy of the meanest girl in camp, who also turned out to have magical powers. *Great, just great.*

Hilla and Kevrina strode into the tent. Kevrina made straight for her, while Hilla used a stream of purple light to knock her brother off his pillow. Grabbing it, she dragged it over to where she could observe the show and sat down.

Kevrina advanced upon Eiryenne as she struggled to get free of the pillow. "You're out of your league, missy. Don't bother putting up a fight."

Eiryenne frowned. Out of your league meant being around powerful mages like Danzi and Tairung. She'd been out of her league for the past several months. Compared to them, Kevrina wasn't a threat. She was just an annoyance.

Eiryenne watched as Kevrina opened her mouth, and a fresh burst of pinkish light reached out for Eiryenne. But the girl shook her magic free of the enchanted pillow and encased herself in a barrier, pillow and all, to block the attack. Then she concentrated on the feeling of free-fall, of plummeting through the sky through stormy clouds in a dragon's claws. The pillow became as weightless as the clouds, and she sank right through it just as Riard walked back in.

"What's this?" he demanded. "Kevrina, back to your seat!"

The pillow was now free of her, but Eiryenne didn't feel like sitting on it again. She sat on the floor as Kevrina walked by and sat down on a large pillow next to Hilla.

"All right," Riard said. He sat on his desk again. "Now, this next topic's mostly for the senior section. Amulets."

Eiryenne glanced at Kevrina, who looked smug. Danzi's amulet glinted on her wrist, along with Eiryenne's glass bead. Both were smeared with pink paint.

"Now, an amulet is defined as a particular type of magical object," Riard said. "Unlike other enchanted objects, an amulet functions independently of the mage who created it. They are also usually limited in function. Most often, they'll just have one specific use.

"Now, the way you make an amulet is by enchantment, but you break off the connection with yourself. Amulets are special because they can be used by just about anybody; it's a premade spell sitting inside a physical container, complete with source magic. It just needs to be activated, usually by a specific word. Now, amulets always have a limited number of uses because their supply of magic is limited to what the actual amulet contains."

Eiryenne thought back to the cooling amulet she used in Danzi's cave and how much more effective it was compared with the warming amulet. Either it had been used a lot less or it had been crafted by a less talented mage.

"The effectiveness of an amulet will also depend on the skill of the mage who creates it," Riard said, as if reading her mind. "Now, an amulet can take on many shapes, but the most common is usually a metal charm on a small chain —"

"Like this?" Kevrina held out her wrist.

Riard looked at it carefully. A few of the older elves murmured amongst themselves. "Yes, exactly like that," he said. "Oh, the craftsmanship on that is beautiful. Where did you get it?"

Kevrina smiled. "It was a gift."

"I see. Now, I want each of you to pick a stone and try turning it into an amulet." He looked up at the younger mages. "Senior section stays. The rest of you can go. This is probably too advanced for most of you."

Leo caught up with Eiryenne once they were outside the tent.

"I don't think I've seen anyone get out of one of Kevrina's traps so quickly before," he said. "That was pretty cool."

"You could have mentioned that she was a mage," Eiryenne said, though inwardly she felt stupid for not scanning her with mage vision herself.

"You didn't ask." Leo shrugged. "But yeah, she's been doing that kind of stuff for a few weeks now, ever since she learned how to enchant fabric. Before that it was pseudo-poisons. Be glad you missed that stage."

"Pseudo-poisons. Sounds exciting." Eiryenne rolled her eyes. "What's next?"

"Combat practice."

They walked down the central path, making their way up to the combat arena. Eiryenne paused. "Wait. Kevrina stole my sword and dagger yesterday. I'll probably need them for this, won't I?"

Leo looked uncertain. "I'm sure they'll have spares."

Eiryenne turned and marched in the direction of her cabin. "Maybe they do. But I've got something to prove."

It was only a few minutes later that she rejoined Leo. Instead of a sword in her hand, she had a smoking burn.

"Magical booby traps," she said when Leo opened his mouth. "Don't ask." She'd rushed in unprepared, and she'd paid the price. Lesson learned.

There were already some people in the arena when Leo and Eiryenne walked in. She recognized a few people from their magic class, as well as the stout boy she had meals with, Grindt.

Grindt was sparring with a tall, thin man dressed in a black tunic. He had a thin salt-and-pepper beard and a thick brown moustache that wound its way across his face. He wielded the biggest broadsword Eiryenne had ever seen, it was over five feet long, far bigger even than Danzi's. It had a plain steel hilt with metal wire wrapped around the two-handed grip. It must have weighed a lot, but the man made it look feather light. He parried Grindt's strikes with superhuman speed, beating down the boy's weapon before he had a chance even to come close to him.

Grindt, who swung a very wide, short sword with a triangular tip, looked tired. He struck this way and that, but still the man blocked him.

"You're trying to win this based on speed, Grindt," the older warrior said. He stepped back and lowered his sword away from the panting boy. "That's not your stronghold. Use your strength and your weight to your advantage instead. Don't just put your arm behind the blade; use your whole body to deliver the blow."

"I'll try that." Grindt nodded. Then he tucked in his arms and charged.

"That's Stroman," Leo said to Eiryenne. "He's our combat instructor. He also happens to be the best swordsman in the entire Resistance."

"Then why did Hurraine leave him behind?" she replied quietly, watching Stroman continue to spar with Grindt.

"Maybe he wanted him to stay and pass his skills along. There's also the fact that he doesn't have any magic," Leo added.

"No magic? But he can't be human, can he?" she muttered. Stroman finished sparring with Grindt and now began to cross swords with an elven youth. He easily matched the elf's speed.

"I heard that he's half-human," Leo said. He took his sword out of his pack and strapped it to his belt. "And half-elf. So, he inherited an elf's strength and speed but didn't luck out when it came to the magic."

Eiryenne spent the next two hours practicing weapons work. Stroman found an extra short sword for her to use, but it felt strange in her grip; she'd gotten too used to her Bremian blade. From there they moved on to spears. Stroman would demonstrate some moves, have them repeat them, and then practice them on each other. Then he moved to drilling them on knife fighting before ending with a little hand-to-hand combat.

It was then that Eiryenne realized just how much work was still ahead of her. Danzi's crash course on sword work and combat had been enough to get her through their journey alive, but it lacked many of the more refined skills and even skipped over some of the fundamentals. She knew most of the basics, but nearly everyone she faced ended up beating her; she simply couldn't match the elves' speed. Grindt was clumsy but strong. If she let her guard down, he could knock her off her feet with one blow. When it came to the other weapons, she was well behind everyone, having had no former training with them. But Stroman assured her that with enough practice, she'd be able to polish up her existing skills, build new ones, and catch up to the others. Maybe she'd never be a master with the sword, but then again, she didn't have to be. Her specialty was healing, after all.

The senior members of their magic class joined them about an hour in. Eiryenne kept her guard up, but Kevrina and her gang appeared to have tired of their little games with the newcomer and instead showed off their weapons skills. Eiryenne found that she'd been hoping Kevrina didn't know how to handle a sword, but she saw that the older girl was quite effective with her short, hooked blade. Hilla, too, was no pushover at any of the weapons; even the elves had trouble with her at knife-fighting. She wasn't afraid to get her hands dirty in hand-to-hand combat, either, and pummelled the dummies with great ferocity.

Cassandra, Taymel, and Mels, on the other hand, were even clumsier with the spear than Eiryenne was, and their sword fighting skills were nonexistent. Rolling their eyes and frequently adjusting their hair, they kept on complaining about how this wasn't what girls were supposed to be doing.

Toward the end of the practice, once Stroman declared that they were done for the day, Eiryenne had a brief moment of respite. She sighed and put her spear down on the ground, her arms aching.

Cassandra's giggles made her open her eyes. She glanced down to see that her spear, along with the sword next to it, had sunk into the dirt by about four inches. Groaning, she began to try to pull them out. They refused to budge.

Still laughing, the girls left the arena as the class began to disperse.

"Hey, Leo," she called as he walked by, weapon pack over his shoulder. "Can you give me a hand?"

Leo hesitated. He was about to follow Roben and Nur out of the arena. Then he caught sight of something beyond the entrance and hurried over to her.

"Sure," he said eagerly, but he wasn't looking at the spear as he took hold of it and pulled, unsuccessfully.

Eiryenne looked over his shoulder as the chattering in the arena quieted.

Danzi strode in through the gate. He'd taken off his cloak, and the blood was gone from his reddish-brown jacket. He gave them and the other teens a quick glance before heading over to Stroman.

"Got any strong silpolish?" he asked.

"How strong?" Stroman looked him over, his eyes lingering on Danzi's sword.

"Something that can get rid of Ucer blood."

"Ah, that stuff's really corrosive," Stroman said with a frown. "I'm surprised your sword is still holding together." He looked thoughtful. "What kind of steel is it? May I see?"

Danzi frowned, but he evidently didn't think that the magic-less man was a threat, so he slid his longsword out of its sheath and handed it to Stroman.

The combat instructor lifted Danzi's sword and turned the blade over in the sun. "I've never seen metal like this in my life," he muttered. "The Ucer blood's not even corroding it yet, just staining for now ... should be fine if you get it off soon. I think we have just the right thing for this." He then glanced at the handle, inlaid with gold and with one ruby at the centre of the cross guard, and another on the pommel. "Beautiful craftsmanship." He ran a finger over the golden guard. "But old. Nine hundred years, at least. Early Belorian if I'm not mistaken."

Danzi reached out and took the sword from him. "If you could find that silpolish, then?"

"Right. Just one moment." Stroman disappeared into the door at the back of the arena, and a few minutes later he came out with a small silver bottle. "This should do." He handed Danzi the bottle and stood back. "I think I recognize that sword, sir. It's the one from that old Belorian legend, isn't it?"

Danzi took the bottle with a shrug.

"Since you and I still have our minds, I assume that the curse has been broken."

"It takes a certain kind of blade to channel my power," the dragon mage said. "Whatever its purpose was before, I am its current master."

"And you are?" Stroman looked puzzled.

"Danzi Daggoras." He smirked. "I find it amusing that you have heard of my sword and not of me. Have you been in this force for long?"

The instructor smiled. "My apologies. I only joined up about five years ago," he said. "I grew up a long way away from here, where stories of that sword ran rampant. Now, if you'll excuse me," he turned to the remaining youngsters, who had lingered around to hear them talk, "our lesson finished ten minutes ago. You will be late for lunch. Hurry up!"

Danzi ambled over to a bench near where Eiryenne and Leo were still wrestling with the spear stuck in the ground. He took his sword out and laid it out on the bench, next to which he placed the silver bottle. Taking a rag out of his pocket, he dipped one end in the bottle and then rubbed it against the blade where an ugly streak of brown rust had settled in near the blood groove. The solution bubbled and hissed, clearing away the rust within seconds.

He left it to dry and turned to the kids.

"Who's he?" Danzi gestured to Stroman.

"Combat instructor. His name's Stroman," answered Eiryenne while Leo opened and closed his mouth wordlessly. "He's half-elf and half-human."

"Hrrm." Danzi casually pulled the spear out of the ground, spraying them both with dirt. He turned it over in his hands idly before tossing it to Eiryenne.

The elf boy finally found his voice. "He's also the best swordsman we've got. He's beaten everybody. My dad, Lianos, Hurraine … I've never seen him lose a match."

"Really?" Danzi muttered.

"Leo, you flatter me." Stroman had come up to them to retrieve the silver bottle now that Danzi was done with it.

"Best swordsman, best mage …" Leo looked from one of them to the other. "I'm glad this spear got stuck in the ground."

"You're a mage?" Stroman turned to Danzi. "How are you with a sword, then? I find that when a man can rely on more than just his blade, he might not be as careful with it." He paused. "Forgive me, but I am curious as to the calibre of the swordsman who wields the Holidrun." He bowed his head. "It would be an honour, sir, to cross blades with such a legendary weapon."

Danzi narrowed his eyes. "So, you are challenging me?"

"Indeed."

The dragon mage picked his sword up off the table. "The only way to see whether someone's the best is to take them on yourself."

"I agree."

Danzi raised his sword, but Stroman put up a hand. "No magic, all right? I have no doubt that you could burn me down with one flick of your hand, but that's not the point, now, is it?"

"Very well."

Danzi and Stroman faced each other in the centre of the arena. The dragon mage didn't wait for Stroman to draw his blade. He just charged.

The other man had his weapon out to block the blow so quickly that it was a blur, and their swords hit with a ring. Danzi then swung his blade in a low arc at Stroman's thigh, but the swordsman caught his blade halfway. He parried the blow easily, smoothly transitioning to one of his own—a series of quick, fluid diagonal slices. Danzi was forced to step back to have the room to block them. Then he leaped forward again, bringing his sword down over Stroman's head. The man dodged out of the way and then caught Danzi's sword on his own, twisting the blade until the hilts locked. He then forced the smaller broadsword's blade to slide down his own, making Danzi raise his arm and expose his side. In the blink of an eye, Stroman unhooked his sword and jabbed the dragon mage in the side. But for all his speed, he never lost his control; the tip of his sword stopped when it was touching Danzi's jacket.

Looking surprised, Danzi raised his sword again and began a furious series of cuts and parries, their blades flashing and knocking together with rays of sparks. But while Danzi may have been stronger, it was becoming evident that Stroman was more skilled. He enveloped the dragon mage in elaborate combinations and tricky manoeuvres that Danzi had trouble keeping up with. Then, as the dragon mage parried his cut, Stroman locked their blades together again, sliding them this way and that. With a sudden wrench, he jerked Danzi's sword out of his hands. It fell, spinning end over end, to land in the dust a few feet away.

Caught up in the moment, Danzi raised his disarmed hand, which began to glow red. But Stroman merely bowed.

"An honour," he repeated, breathing heavily.

Still panting, Danzi looked at him for a few seconds. Then he lowered his hand, picked up his sword, and strode out of the arena without another word.

He passed Lianos, who'd just walked in. Lianos came to the centre of the ring and looked at the settling dust.

"You beat Danzi without magic *and* lived to tell the tale? Impressive," he said.

Eiryenne waited a few minutes before she and Leo went out of the arena and came back to the camp for lunch. She knew it was best to avoid Danzi when he was that cross.

Leo was chattering away about the sparring match all the way to the cabins. He and Eiryenne both dropped off their weapons packs at their bunks, though Eiryenne wasn't sure how long hers would stay there, before heading down to catch the last of lunch break.

While they ate, Eiryenne caught a glimpse of Riard arguing about something with an elf dressed in purple and white. She recognized him—Leo's uncle. He gave her a smouldering stare as she passed, and she quickened her step.

After lunch, Riard came by to tell Eiryenne that rather than going to an archery lesson with the elves, she'd be going to embroidery with her cabin mates.

"Embroidery?" she said slowly. "Umm, but I don't really embroider much, you know. Why the switch? Are the archery and language classes too full?"

Riard looked sheepish. "No, but there's been some … some trouble with the class. It's not your fault."

He hurried up and left.

Eiryenne turned to Leo. "Your uncle doesn't teach archery, does he?"

"Er, maybe." Leo looked sheepish.

"He does," said Grindt, slurping up his soup. "I've seen him at it. And Leo's aunt Nultela does the Elvish classes."

Eiryenne turned to Leo. "I don't get it. They've both been giving me evil stares all day. What's the problem?"

Leo didn't answer.

As expected, embroidery was a nightmare. The other girls all sat around in a big tent with needles, thread, and patches of fabric. Perhaps Kevrina planned to bespell Eiryenne's fabric right away, but she found that she didn't have to; she was already as clumsy as could be with the needle. Try as she might, she could not copy the elegant designs that the other girls were producing. She jabbed herself in the finger more times than she could count, and her face grew hot as Cassandra began pointing out the obvious flaws in her designs.

Then they grew tired of berating her and returned to their own conversations, which were, in Eiryenne's opinion, even more strange.

"Did you hear about Lissa and Gordon?"

"Oh my god, you don't actually mean that she's going for that ugly face? What does she see in him?"

"I don't know, but did you *see* the state of her robes today? I mean, honestly, who wears *pink* with *green*. That's just stupid!"

"I think we have an even better example of what not to wear right here, ladies."

Eiryenne ignored them, busying herself with working a knot out of her thread. So far, she was only pulling it tighter. The talk around her continued as the girls discussed fashions, boys, and gossip from around camp. Then they started to complain about the combat lesson and camp life in general.

The more she heard, the less Eiryenne could relate. She felt trapped here in this room with these girls who didn't want her there and treated her like a freak. She suddenly found herself missing the road, where it was only her and Danzi and the horses. Horses she understood. Danzi didn't whisper behind her back or spread rumours; he told her exactly what he thought. He didn't care about what her life was like before or make snide comments about the state of her clothes.

Once again, she doubted her decision to come here.

After a little while, Taymel slid over to sit beside her.

"I don't know how you got that spear out," she said. "It was supposed to strangle you after a few hours then stay in the ground for a week at least. That made them pretty mad. They used up a lot of magic."

Eiryenne shrugged. These little mages had nothing on Danzi.

"I'm glad that I'm no longer the worst at embroidery here," Taymel continued with a light laugh.

Eiryenne looked down at her needlework disaster. She wasn't sure why Taymel was suddenly trying to talk to her.

"So, you fancy anyone in camp yet?"

"Huh?" Eiryenne wasn't really sure what she meant, but she realized that Taymel was just trying to pick up more gossip.

"Okay, forget that." Taymel paused. "What's your favourite outfit?"

"Um, I don't really know," she replied. "I haven't really had much choice out on the road." She paused, listening to the other girls continuing to chatter away. Cassandra, Mels, and Taymel were ordinary humans. Was this what ordinary human girls talked about? Eiryenne realized that she had fewer things in common with them than she did someone like Leo or even Danzi. "Do you always do that?" she asked. "Talk about embroidery and clothes. Make superficial complaints about life, even though you have it a lot better than some of the people I've seen. And your lessons? It's like you don't even care."

Taymel shrugged. "We've all grown up in the camps. Sure, it switches location every few years, but other than that everything stays the same. Why should we care about sword work? That's a boy's job."

"The Emperor's soldiers don't discriminate who they attack," said Eiryenne.

"What soldiers?" Taymel laughed. "We've never been raided. This camp is safe. And it's boring, too."

"But everyone seems so apathetic. During practice, Stroman gave us a pep talk to remind us why we were training and what we're going to fight for. Half the class yawned."

"Again, why should we care?" Taymel shrugged again. "What goes on out there has nothing to do with us. I don't believe half the reports that come in, anyway."

"Then why are you all even here?" Eiryenne demanded.

"Because this is where our lovely, delusional parents decided to raise us," said Taymel with a smirk.

They'd had a sheltered life here, Eiryenne realized. They didn't care about the war. This wasn't their cause by choice; it was theirs by inheritance. They had no reason to believe in this fight.

Having been in the thick of the Empire's chaos and experienced first-hand what kinds of destruction the Resistance stood against, Eiryenne found herself utterly disgusted by what she heard.

"I was wrong, then," she muttered. "This isn't the next generation of soldiers. It's the next generation of losers and cowards."

As soon as the words were out of her mouth, Eiryenne knew she was in trouble. Kevrina and the other girls fell silent, glowering.

"*What* did you just say?" demanded Hilla.

"Losers? You're calling *us* losers?" burst out Cassandra. "You're the one who dresses like a bum savage, can't embroider to save your life, and *you dare* to think that you're better than us?"

"You pig," sneered Kevrina, getting up. "Pathetic, good-for-nothing freak."

Kevrina muttered something, and the fabric around Eiryenne's hands suddenly snaked around her fingers to envelop her in makeshift handcuffs.

"You're nothing," Kevrina said. "You've got no friends and no talent." The fabric handcuffs began to burn Eiryenne's skin. More fabric twisted its way to her neck. "You don't deserve to be here. It's no wonder they can't stand having you in their class."

Eiryenne's cheeks burned. She tried to tell herself that their words meant nothing, but each insult fed into her own underlying insecurities.

There was a jab of truth there, and it hurt. Suddenly she was the same orphaned, unwanted feral child from the little village. She tried to open her mouth, but her confidence had plummeted, and no words came out, just a strangled squeak.

The girls shook their heads and laughed. Eiryenne looked pleadingly toward Taymel, but she was laughing along with the rest of them.

Then Hilla and Kevrina began to chant together, and the strand of fabric around her neck began to tighten and burn.

Eiryenne felt like the bottom had just dropped out of her stomach. The sight and feeling stirred up a memory, a memory she thought she had buried out of sight. But it all came back to her: the Necklace around her throat, burning and getting tighter until Tairung completely decapitated her in that awful nightmare. As the fabric around her neck squeezed tighter, it seemed to squeeze out all her courage and newfound identity, leaving her with nothing but a shattered frame of terror. She screamed. To her ears, their high-pitched peals of laugher echoed with a thousand demons' voices.

You thought you'd gotten away.

She struggled against the ropes, her entire body flailing, her arms madly clutching at the enchanted fabric.

But I'm always here. Waiting in the corners of your mind.

"Um, guys." Taymel had stopped laughing. Watching the pure terror on Eiryenne's face had been funny for a few minutes, but now that it had turned to panic, she couldn't help but feel a stab of pity. "Maybe that's enough. I think she learned her lesson."

"Enough?" Kevrina cackled. "What's the matter, can't stomach it? Want to be next, then?"

"No, I mean," Taymel stuttered. "She's so scared, I bet she'll run right out of the camp. Wouldn't that be funny? Let's let her go."

"Yeah, good idea," Hilla said. "Time to go hunting, girls." She snapped her fingers, and the fabric around Eiryenne fell to the ground. "Twenty cronos says I bag her first." She put down her embroidery needles and reached around her belt to grab a long, hooked knife.

Kevrina grinned. "You're on."

By now Eiryenne couldn't hear them. As the pressure around her neck fell away, she fell forward, gasping for air. But her legs were already moving. She ran blindly, tearing through walls of tents and over fences. Behind her she could hear footsteps, amplified by her fears into demonic hoofbeats.

There was no room for thoughts in her brain as the panic blacked out her rational mind. Overcome by fear, she turned to an impulse that had been ingrained in her subconscious over the course of the past several months: when in danger, run to the fire.

She came upon a strand of it and zeroed in its unmistakable signal. Her heart pounding, she kept on running until she crashed through a door and tumbled, head over heels, to come to rest on the floor.

There was a scrape of something wooden above her. Eiryenne looked up to see Danzi and Lianos seated at an iron-wrought table, both staring at her.

Danzi was frowning slightly. "Another one?" he said, noting her panic attack. "I thought you were done with them, girl."

Lianos opened his mouth to add something, but just then Kevrina, Hilla, and Cassandra burst into the cabin, Taymel and Mels hot on their heels. Upon seeing who was at the table, they slid to an abrupt halt. The triumphant expression on the two lead girls' faces quickly faded as they looked from one dragon mage to the other.

Danzi glanced at Hilla. She shrank away. Then he turned his amber gaze upon Kevrina. She pursed her lips but stood her ground.

Behind her, Taymel was dragging Cassandra back.

"It's the dragon's den," she hissed. "Are you crazy?"

Danzi's frown deepened as he looked over Kevrina. He slowly got up and stepped over Eiryenne until he was facing the other girl.

He took an audible sniff. "Another human mage?" he rumbled; his voice laced with disdain. Something was familiar about Kevrina. Something he really didn't like. "Which lineage, I wonder?"

Kevrina began to back away, but Danzi grabbed her wrist, his hand a dragon paw. He pulled it forward roughly, exposing the warming amulet and glass bead that she had stolen from Eiryenne. Both were painted bright pink.

"This belongs to me." Danzi ripped them off her arm, and fire burst into life amidst his claws. The pink layer burned. Kevrina jumped back with a start, rubbing her wrist.

He raised the amulet, now cleaned of its paint, and slid it into his pocket. He then looked at the bead. "This doesn't." He tossed it to Eiryenne.

The glass was hot; she dropped it onto the floor in front of her as it cooled, steam rising from its surface.

Without another word, the girls turned and ran out.

Lianos rose to his feet and closed the door. "People never knock any more," he muttered.

Eiryenne picked up the cooling bead, which was still warm. But it was a comfortable warmth now. And not only had Danzi's fire burned away that foul pink paint, but it had also taken off years of dirt and grime that even soap couldn't remove. The bead gleamed in her hand; its surface as spotless as the day it was made. She slid it into her pocket, since the leather band it had been strung on had been burned to ashes.

Danzi returned to the table, still looking cross.

"*You're fine with Eiryenne,*" Lianos said in Draconic. "*What does Kevrina matter?*"

"*I accepted that a few unrelated pockets may have survived,*" Danzi replied. "*But Kevrina looks to be one of his.*"

"*You barely know her,*" Lianos replied with a shrug.

"*But she means I didn't finish the job.*"

"*Come on, Brother. Surely you have overcome your prejudices by now.*"

Danzi gritted his teeth. "*Old habits die hard.*" He turned to Eiryenne and switched back to Common. "Now, what's this with you having a panic attack in the middle of camp?" He bent down and helped her up, grabbing her by the elbow and steering her to the bench next to him. "You went toe-to-toe with soldiers, wolves, and Tairung and kept your cool. Now you're scared of a bunch of teenagers?" He shook his head. "I'll never understand you humans."

Eiryenne took a few deep breaths until her heart steadied. Then she spoke. "They did this … this … fabric spell thing and it-it reminded me of that nightmare with Tairung. The one after Balon's castle. And I'm not sure what happened next but, I lost it."

"Hrrm." Danzi looked disappointed. "I thought you were tougher than that by now."

Lianos shrugged. "Flashbacks. Happens to the best of us." He glanced at Danzi meaningfully.

"I heard him talking," Eiryenne mumbled.

Danzi gave her a look. "I made quite sure that there were no demonic traces left in you," he said. "Your only enemy is fear." He rose to his feet and went to the door.

"Where are you going?" Lianos asked.

"Hunting." Danzi strode out into the air and transformed.

Lianos sighed. "Oh, boy." He got up as well. "I better go keep an eye on him," he said to Eiryenne. "And you'll have to go, too. I'm locking up."

There were no lights other than a small candle, so it was hard to make out anything else besides the table and the door. Eiryenne decided that she wanted to return here in daylight sometime. She was curious to see what kinds of interesting things Lianos kept in his cabin.

She followed him out. Eiryenne hadn't realized how dark it had gotten, but it was already well into the evening. She found that she didn't feel like going to dinner. And the last place she wanted to be that night was her own cabin.

Eiryenne thought back to her initial tour with Leo. Half the cabins were empty. Trouble was, with everyone away at dinner, she wasn't sure which ones those were.

"Lianos, do you think I could stay in one of the empty cabins?" she said.

There was a flicker of blue fire as he locked the door. "I guess you could," he said. "But keep in mind that the army can return at any time, and you wouldn't want to be caught in the wrong person's bunk."

"Can you show me the right one, then?"

Lianos looked thoughtful. Then he sighed. "That one over there, two rows over. Straw roof, leather gutters. Keep an ear out for the horns."

"Thanks."

"And keep in mind," he continued. "this is temporary. You'll have to face them sooner or later."

As she walked to the empty cabin, Eiryenne decided she wished it was later instead of sooner. Then she heard the light swish of dragon wings on the air. She turned, but Lianos was already gone. Which was too bad because she was getting rather curious about his dragon form. She decided she was going to catch him in it one of these days.

5 ~ In the Dragon's Shadow

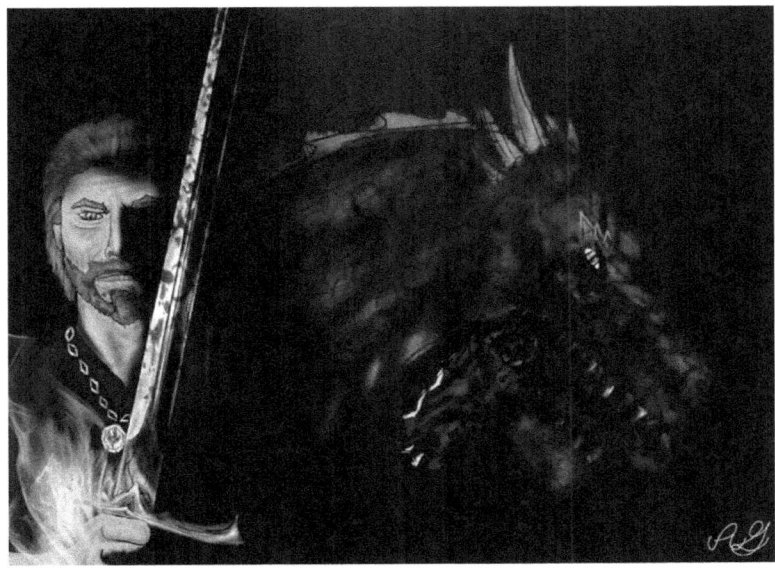

She got up early the next morning, as always. Her muscles ached from a combination of combat practice and crashing through tents, but she made herself get up and do her morning exercises. Danzi was nowhere to be seen, so she did them by herself, keeping out of sight by Lianos's cabin.

When the breakfast bell finally rang, she stepped carefully onto the path. The last thing she wanted to do was face Kevrina and Hilla again, but her stomach growled, demanding food. And she knew that if today was going to be as action-packed as the day before, she couldn't afford to miss more meals.

A little way down the path, Leo was walking to breakfast with Roben and Nur. Eiryenne ducked behind a tent to avoid them. She didn't feel like talking right now.

"So, is hanging out with her worth it?" Nur asked.

"It so was yesterday," Leo replied. "I got to see Stroman swordfight with Danzi. It was really cool. But I gotta say, she's different than what

I expected. She doesn't talk about her adventures that much. And when she does, it's like she regrets even doing it. I don't get it."

"You better pull your head out of the sand, man." Roben shook his head. "Half the camp could hear your aunt and uncle shouting at you last night. It sounds like they're threatening to disown you if you go near her or Danzi again."

Leo shrugged. "Whatever. We never get anything exciting happening here. And now that it has, I'm not letting it get away from me. Besides, they'll let up when Dad comes back."

"What if he doesn't?"

Eiryenne waited a few seconds before continuing out. But a few tents before the meal tent, Leo spotted her and broke away from the group.

"Hey. Good morning!" he said, grinning.

"Morning," she mumbled.

"I hope you're in the mood to talk, because I'd love to hear some more details about the Empire over breakfast," he said.

"Leo, I've told you all I'm going to," she said.

"Oh, and I've always wondered …" Leo carried on as if he hadn't heard her. "Have you killed anyone?"

Eiryenne grimaced, remembering the soldiers ambushing them at the Cavern. She nodded.

Leo's jaw dropped. "Whoa. That's really cool. What's it like?"

She frowned. "It's horrible. Why would you possibly want to know what it's like?"

Leo frowned. "I've been stuck in these camps my entire life. Been always hearing these stories of these people going out in the world and doing amazing things. You're lucky that you got to experience some of that so early. So why are you talking about all this like you'd rather not have done it?"

"Of *course* I'd rather not have done it," she burst out. "How can you talk like that about taking people's lives? There is *nothing* fun about killing or watching it happen. You might have grown up on these tales about how things are like out there." She paused, thinking of Hayden's storybook and how wrong it ended up being. "You might have been told that it's glorious and amazing. But believe me, once you get out there, and you see the things that steel and claws can do to a body, and you can smell the corpses rotting, then you'll realize the truth. And unless you're anything like Danzi, the last thing on your mind is fun."

The elf boy studied her for a second. "Some people think it's fun. I bet Danzi does."

"You're *nothing* like Danzi," she retorted. "You're too ...," she almost said *huma,*. "too careful. And I don't think you should want to be like him. Danzi is cruel. He's sadistic, selfish, and heartless. He doesn't value the lives of others." She paused, blinking. What she said was true. It was wrong to admire him. "He likes killing, yes. And he enjoys it because it's the only thing he has."

Leo hesitated. Then he turned away. "I knew you were no fun," he muttered. He walked over to his friends. "You were right about her," he said to Roben.

Nur put his hand on Leo's shoulder. "Come on," he said. "Let's go before Kevrina puts a spell at us, too. You know how that lot think, guilty by association." He shot Eiryenne a look before they headed off.

Eiryenne sighed. She wasn't sure what had caused that outburst. Though she hadn't known Leo that long, she already considered him a friend. He was one of the few people at the camp that had welcomed her from the start. And the idea of him growing up to follow in Danzi's footsteps, well, it had rubbed her the wrong way. Leo could do a lot of good with his life if he chose to. The last thing this world needed was another Danzi.

She took her plate and walked through the rows of tents, searching for a place to sit. Grindt was gone from their usual table and there was an acrid smell of smoke coming from the bench. Eiryenne could hear him screaming somewhere in the north end of the camp.

Another prank gone wrong.

She avoided the smoking table and kept walking, ignoring the snide comments that came from Kevrina's table. As she passed them, she could see two of the girls, along with Tukse, get up and follow her.

"Get out of here, you freak," someone at Kevrina's table muttered.

"No one wants you here. Go back to that pigsty you crawled out of."

There were murmurs of agreement and several chuckles. Eiryenne blushed despite herself. She tried to tell herself that their words didn't matter; their opinions were meaningless. But somehow their remarks still stung.

There was nowhere to sit. The other tables were all full. Faces turned to look at her and then whisper behind closed hands to their neighbours, undoubtedly describing last night's escapade. Eiryenne turned away, starting to get a little bit desperate. She needed to find shelter from this hostile crowd.

Then she spotted Danzi, who had an iron-wrought table all to himself at the edge of the cluster. People took detours to avoid walking past it, and the neighbouring tables emptied quickly as elves and shapeshifters alike gave him nervous glances before gobbling down their food.

Eiryenne wondered whether Danzi had once been like Leo, young and filled with dreams of grandeur. What was it that had set him on this path?

Eiryenne hesitated. She wasn't sure how Danzi would react if she sat at his table. It would have been embarrassing if he just got up and left. Even worse if he told her to leave.

But she realized he would do neither. He wouldn't want to show that a mere human girl was enough of a bother. Suddenly, she was sure that he would do nothing at all.

She strode over to Danzi's table and sat down, far away enough to avoid crowding him but not so far as to appear perched on the opposite end of the table. The tables around them fell silent.

"Hi," she said brightly.

Danzi ignored her. He was bored. He'd already stayed here longer than he planned. But the package he was waiting for still hadn't arrived. He wished it would hurry up and get here so that he could snatch it and go on taking the Empire apart, piece by piece. He didn't like sitting idle. Riard had advised him to avoid transforming when possible; it would agitate an already tense situation, he'd said. Danzi sighed and took another bite of his steak.

Satisfied that she'd be able to have her meal here in peace, Eiryenne stuffed some of the omelette into her mouth. It was delicious. The eggs reminded her of the ones that she'd eaten on her trip here. Danzi had caught a large, silvery blue beast that looked like a fish with legs. Its eggs had tasted a bit like these.

This gave her an idea. Maybe Danzi still wasn't one for idle conversation, but perhaps he'd answer knowledge-related questions.

"Do you know what these are?" she asked, pointing to the eggs. "Haverick eggs, like last week?"

"No. Haverick eggs have more orange around the middle," he said, pointing to the ring of yellowy purple that sat in the middle of the egg white. "These are Odonton."

Eiryenne looked up. Kevrina's gang had returned to their table. She gave Kevrina a smug look, as if daring her to try anything with a dragon at her table.

Kevrina frowned at her. She turned up her nose and muttered something in Tukse's ear. Cassandra and Mels were chattering away, but Kevrina continued to eat in a subdued silence. Behind them, Leo was staring at her. Then Roben nudged him and said something. Leo looked back at his plate, shaking his head. People at the other tables were giving them strange glances, too, but no one dared to approach.

Eiryenne smiled to herself. Kevrina couldn't do a thing under the dragon mage's nose. Danzi may not have been very talkative, but he was great for scaring away unpleasant people. She hoped that he'd remain at the camp for a little longer, though inwardly she knew he wasn't likely to linger.

She reached over and tapped Danzi's mug. "Poisoned again?"

He smirked. "Nope, which means that everyone went through their poison inventory last night and failed to find a suitable toxin."

"No wonder they're all in such a bad mood."

A few minutes later, Riard came to lean on their table.

"What's taking him so long?" Danzi asked. "I'm getting restless."

"I don't know. He should've been here yesterday. I'd tell you to go out and intercept him, but there's no telling what route he took."

"I'm tired of waiting, Riard."

Riard frowned. "You and me both. The quicker you get out of here, the better. This is a very uneasy truce you made with the Council — technically, you're still a trespasser in the camp. We've never had this kind of situation before, and the councillors are getting jumpier with every day you spend here. Everyone is."

Just then another man came up to their table. Eiryenne recognized him from their arrival — he was the one who'd spat a curse upon Danzi when they came. There were even more bones intertwined among his black dreadlocks now.

"Your days are numbered, dragon," he growled at Danzi. "You know that as soon as the victorious Hurraine returns with our war mages, she will destroy you. And there won't be anything you can do about it."

"Go find some more bones to obsess over, Urdak," Danzi retorted. "Before I decide that I need another appetizer."

"Convenient, isn't it?" Urdak drawled. "You come back right when all our good mages are out fighting. A little too convenient, I think."

"Don't start anything you can't finish," Danzi said quietly with the edge of a growl in his voice.

"That's enough!" Riard saw the glint in Danzi's eye and grabbed the other man by the shoulder. "I am *not* having a brawl first thing in the morning. That's a Council order. Understood?"

Urdak gave them another glare before slowly walking off.

Riard sighed, wiping sweat off his brow. "See what I mean?" he said, exasperated. Then he headed away.

The rest of their meal went by without interruptions. Eiryenne knew she was safe at this table, but she also knew that Lianos was right; she couldn't run forever. She'd have to go face her tormentors sooner or later.

"Danzi," she began. "What if, there's someone you want to beat but you can't, because they're stronger and more skilled. What do you do?" She didn't imagine that it was a problem he'd ever had, but the dragon mage looked thoughtful.

"What you do with any enemy," he said. "Do your research. Get to know their tactics. Exploit them. Find an advantage. Press it. And of course, strengthen your own weaknesses. Train." He paused. "Try it. Good practice for when you're out there on the battlefield for real." Danzi paused, looking at her more closely. "It's time you took matters into your own hands."

He looked up at something in the distance. There was a boy coming through the camp gate dressed in a messenger's lightweight clothes. He was carrying a package wrapped in yellow paper.

"Finally," Danzi breathed. Then he transformed, and the red dragon bounded forward, closing in on the boy within seconds. He ignored the shouts and screams and fired spells, grabbing the package firmly in his jaws and then taking to the sky.

With a few sweeps of his powerful wings, he quickly faded away into the clouds.

Eiryenne let out the breath she was holding. So that was it, then. Danzi was gone, off on another one of his crazy adventures, trying to overturn the Empire in his own way.

***

"You'd be surprised at how much information you can find in books," Riard said. He passed another dusty volume to Eiryenne and had her struggle through an obscure paragraph on ancient parchment-making.

Ever since the embroidery disaster, Eiryenne had balked at going to another class. Instead, she asked Riard to tutor her in the art of reading and writing. Elvish she needed for spells. And as for Common, Eiryenne looked at the wall of books. She was starting to form a plan. And she needed both languages to research it.

They started with an old manuscript on Kive customs; it was very dry, so she was glad when they switched volumes and Riard had her try a small excerpt from *The Book of Beasts*. It was an encyclopaedia of sorts, listing facts about all the different magical creatures of Shotang.

"Choose any one creature and read its entry out loud," he told her.

"Hmm." She skimmed through the pages, deciding she'd probably try to find out more about a creature that somehow pertained to her — like dragons, for instance. But then, as she flipped the page, searching for the dragon entry, something caught her eye. It was a small drawing done in silvery ink on the edge of the parchment: a dazzling white horse with a horn coming from its forehead.

Thinking back to the unicorn horn Danzi used to banish Tairung from her, she paused.

"The unicorn," she read. "Pale, graceful equines with a single horn. Fifteen to seventeen hands high. Coat colours can range from a dusky grey to bright silver or white. Horn colours are gold, white, silver, crème, and any variant of such." She paused. This wasn't giving her the answers she was looking for. She glanced farther down the paragraph. "Unicorns are considered the most powerful magical healers in Shotang. Their abilities in combating injury and poison are unparalleled. It is said that even after a unicorn's death, its horn continues to naturally cleanse anything tainted by poison or demonic magic. For this reason, horns are highly sought after by poachers, and unicorns themselves decree any attempted poaching the highest sacrilege, punishable by death." She paused. "But a unicorn's magic is only as pure as their soul. If a unicorn starts to become corrupted, their powers begin to change, and this poison-clearing function disappears." No wonder Tairung's horn chip in the Necklace had no such powers.

"Good pronunciation," Riard said. "Keep reading."

"Unicorns live together in herds and feed off grass and other low-growing vegetation. They can live on plains or in valleys. The Valley of Peace harbours the main population in Shotang." Eiryenne skimmed down again. "Wars—none recent, only two of historical importance—with the demons and with the ... dragons." She stopped, frowning. Was this how Danzi had gotten his hands on a unicorn horn—a wartime trophy?

"Good, good," Riard said distractedly.

The sounds of girls' voices from outside the cabin brought Eiryenne's thoughts back to the camp and her more immediate issues.

"Riard, why do they hate me?" she said abruptly.

"Oh, don't be silly," he said distractedly. "Nobody hates you. Now, on page twenty-three—"

"But they do. There are far more diverse people at this camp, but I'm treated like the biggest freak of all."

Riard sat back and brushed his hair out of his eyes. "It's not you, per se. People are judging you by your association with Danzi. It's not your fault." He sighed. "That dragon is such a controversial figure around here that, for better or for worse, all of his associates must face those prejudices." And as he looked at the ground, Eiryenne realized that he meant himself as well. Danzi stirred up turbulence wherever he went, and at camp Riard was the one who had to straighten it all out.

"He must have done something really big," she muttered. "But no one tells me what it is. Not exactly. All I get are these strange rumours."

"All I can say is that some years ago, his actions strongly affected everyone in this force," Riard said. "It's all we've been able to do just to keep it together since then."

Eiryenne sighed. Just when she thought she'd had all the answers, it was just like the Necklace all over again. Too many mysteries. No answers.

Because the burning question that she wanted answered was this: who was Danzi Daggoras, really? She'd travelled with him for months, and everywhere she'd seen ripples, shadows of things he'd done. But what exactly had it been?

It occurred to her that perhaps, just as with the Necklace, some things were better left unknown.

There was a quick knock at the door, a rapid array of taps. Then it swung open, and in walked a tall, full-grown elf man Eiryenne hadn't seen before. He was wearing a long, flowing tunic with yellow and green designs under and over a fine chain mail shirt. There was an empty quiver slung over his shoulder, along with an enormous longbow.

"Riard," he said. "I can barely believe my ears. I just spoke with Lianos, and he says that I just missed the red dragon himself."

"Unbelievable, isn't it?" said the mage, looking thoughtful. "Anyway, good to see you back, Yolen. I'm not sure what you told your boy, but he's been absolutely ecstatic over Danzi's visit." He turned to Eiryenne. "We'll wrap up for today. The archery range should be free by now. Go practice there until lunch."

Eiryenne left them and headed to the range. The archery instructor, Leo's uncle, had just packed up and left, but she spotted Leo and a few of his friends still shooting. She walked up to them.

"Got an extra bow, anyone?" she said.

"Why, what happened to yours?" Roben said with a smirk.

"Broke it over an ogre's head," she replied, trying to sound casual.

"Good enough for me." Leo put down his bow and then rummaged around the canvas bag at their feet. "Here, you can try my old one." He handed Eiryenne a beautifully carved wooden bow with an engraved ivory grip and a supple, sinewy string.

Eiryenne tested the string. She hadn't shot a bow since the fight at the cavern, and this fine longbow was a far cry from the old hunting bow of Hayden's that she was used to shooting. She strung it with some difficulty then nocked an arrow and aimed. There were several bales of hay downrange, each with charcoal-smudged circles as targets. Each bull's eye already contained a handful of the elves' arrows.

She aimed as best as she could then took a breath and shot. The arrow flew to embed itself in the dirt beside the hay bale. Ignoring the elves' sniggers, Eiryenne drew another arrow and shot some more until she had a feel for the weapon. Finally, her next few shots made it a few inches from the bull's eye before hitting it in full.

Roben and Nur looked impressed. "Not bad," Nur said. "For a human."

Eiryenne smiled and reached for another arrow. Archery was the one thing apart from healing for which she had a natural talent. It was also the only thing that Danzi hadn't given her lessons in. She'd never seen him so much as touch a bow. Not that he needed one.

Her arms hurt from using the powerful bow. Eiryenne lowered it then turned to see the elf from Riard's cabin, Yolen, walking up to them.

"Hey, Dad." Leo ran up to him. "Did you hear? Danzi came by."

"Yes, so I've heard," Yolen said.

So, this was Leo's dad. As Eiryenne looked from one of them to the other, she decided that she did see some similarities in their faces. Both had long, straight cheekbones and light green eyes. Yolen's hair was a shade lighter than his son's, though, and a lot longer, bound back in a ponytail to avoid tangling in his chain mail.

"I even got to talk to him and everything," Leo continued. "And this," he jabbed a finger at Eiryenne, "this is Eiryenne. She travelled with Danzi on that Necklace quest."

"I see." Yolen gave Eiryenne a quick glance, noting the bow in her hands. "You've never held an Elvish bow before, have you?"

"No. My old one broke before I came here, so—"

"You just said that you broke it over an ogre's head," Leo said slowly. "Why, did you run out of arrows?"

"Yup."

"So, what happened to the ogre? And how many arrows did you get into him before you ran out?"

Yolen put a hand on Leo's shoulder. "Leo, be polite," he chided. "It's not fair to Eiryenne to barrage her with questions all the time. Treat her like a person, not a storybook."

The elf boy looked at the ground. "Sorry."

Yolen looked back at the girl. "Now, I hear there's been a problem with the archery instructors?"

"Sort of."

The elf man picked up his bow. "Then let's get started."

After an hour of being drilled on Elvish firing techniques, Eiryenne's arms felt like they were going to fall off. Nonetheless, she was glad finally to be getting some proper training with her favourite weapon.

Leo didn't say much during lunch, probably because they were sitting within earshot of his dad. Eiryenne's thoughts wandered as she ate.

Riard was right. So far, everyone here either liked or disliked her based on their attitude toward Danzi. By the looks of things, Riard and Yolen were old allies of his, and Leo had grown up on a version of legends about the red dragon that differed from what everyone else in the camp seemed to know. Leo only liked hanging out with her because he hoped to snatch some tidbit or another about the dragon or the supposedly glorious life outside these walls. Now that his dad had shut him up, it was no wonder he had nothing to say.

"Pass the water, please," said Grindt, jerking Eiryenne out of her thoughts. She smiled and passed it to him. At least Grindt and Stroman both treated her fairly, and neither had much prior knowledge of Danzi.

Well, it was about time she started making a name for herself here.

6 ~ Carving a New Path

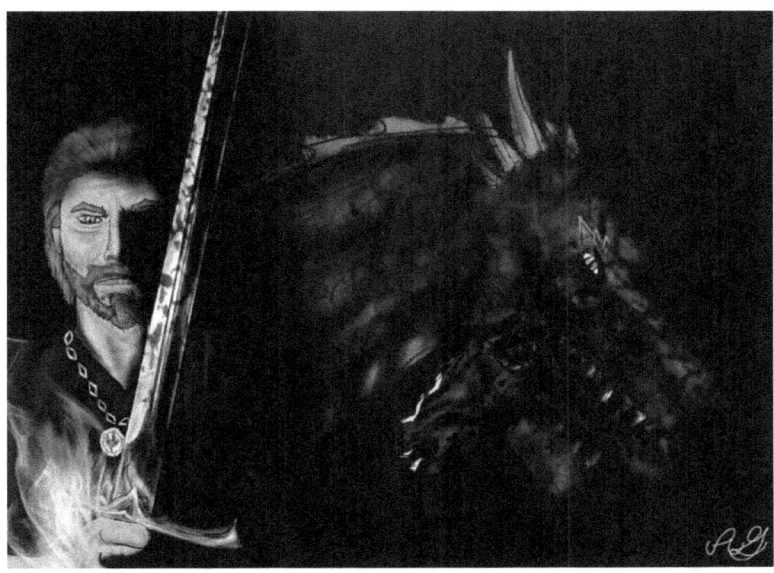

In the afternoons, Eiryenne would head to the stables for her usual chores. It was the end of her second week at camp, and already she'd gotten to ride several great horses. And even when the number of stalls to muck out seemed endless, she knew that she'd been lucky to land herself a chore that she at least partly enjoyed. After her section of the stables was clean, she'd saddle up one of the horses and go for a trail ride in the woods. Mounted combat lessons with Stroman were every second day, so the length of her hack varied. Pretty soon, Yolen started practicing mounted archery with them as well, and her free time was further reduced.

Eiryenne walked down the row of stalls, wondering which horse she'd take out this time. She left a carrot in each of their feed boxes. First was Song, a spirited, feisty little chestnut mare that reminded her of Neil. Next to her was Timor, a flashy paint stallion with white splotches on his brown coat who could turn on a dime but really didn't like cats. Then there was Mystic, a rangy blue roan pony who spooked at everything and couldn't stand having people touch his hooves. On the end of the row were Talluma and Rop, two tall bays that most people considered unrideable.

They weren't the cream of the crop, but they were hers to care for, and she did her best to treat them like they were the finest horses in Shotang.

Eiryenne stopped as she came out of the stables and leaned on the fence of the pasture. She could see Leo out there, catching his horses and taking them in. His lot was similar to hers: a mix of old warhorses, ponies, messenger racers, and general riding horses. There was even the odd pack mule or two. Leo's favourite of the bunch was Tomahawk, a stocky, smoky black stallion with roaning on his flanks. The pattern was known as rabicano, but the horse was named after his ridiculously messy forelock, which tended to stick straight up in the air in sharp spikes, along with most of his mane.

A whinny came from a separate pasture, fenced off from the others. A lone stallion stood there, nostrils flared and calling repeatedly to the other horses. He was an appaloosa with a patch of white on his hindquarters permeated with leopard-like spots. The rest of his coat was a rich light brown, with white marks in his dark brown mane and a V-shaped white streak across his neck. He paced repeatedly back and forth, stomping the ground with heavily feathered legs.

His name was Toperaz, and he was Councillor Molekk's personal parade horse. The problem was Molekk rarely rode him and kept him separate from all the other "common" horses. Eiryenne heard that he was some kind of rare breed and had a pedigree to die for. For Molekk, Toperaz was an object, a symbol of his status, not a living, breathing animal. And the horse suffered for it. Day after day, he was cooped up in his pasture alone. Apart from special feeding sessions, no one was allowed to come near him.

"Are you going out on the trails?"

Eiryenne blinked. Leo was standing in front of her with Tomahawk all tacked up. How he managed to fit that ridiculous hairdo underneath a bridle was beyond her.

"Don't you think it's a pity that that beautiful horse is stuck up there, wasting away?" she said softly.

"Oh, I really don't like the look on your face," Leo muttered.

She looked closer. The horse's breathing was strangely laboured. There was a vine wrapped around Toperaz's neck.

"He's hurt. Look! He's going to strangle himself."

"Don't be stupid, that's Molekk's horse. We've got plenty of others to deal with."

More apathy. Eiryenne took a breath. "You know what? That's the same kind of attitude that leads to all the Empire nonsense out there." She paused. "I came here to fix things that weren't right. And I might as well start with that." Change had to start somewhere. And if there was one thing Danzi had taught her, it was that doing the right thing didn't always mean playing by the rules.

"Keep a lookout," she said to Leo. Then she set off for the high pasture, the grass swishing against her boots.

Toperaz nickered as she approached. The sound reassured her, but Eiryenne's heart was still thundering in her ears as she climbed over the fence and walked up to the big horse.

"Easy, boy," she whispered, slipping her fingers under the vine, and carefully untangling it from his neck.

She patted his shaggy side. The horse's coat was filthy and matted from a lack of grooming. Then Eiryenne looked around. Leo was still where she'd left him, scanning the landscape, but so far, the only beings within eyeshot were the other horses.

Well, she'd come this far. Might as well see this through.

Eiryenne ducked out of the pasture for a halter and lead line, then came back and put them on the horse. She led Toperaz from the pasture as quickly as she dared, tying him up out of sight in the stable courtyard.

Leo came in, panting. "You are out of your mind."

"Get some brushes."

Once she'd gotten Toperaz's coat clean and reasonably shiny, she picked out his hooves and checked a bump on his leg. Satisfied that the horse was healthy, Eiryenne tied him up in an empty stall and went to find a saddle and bridle that would fit him. Before long, she was leading him out the back to where Leo was waiting on Tomahawk.

The elf raised an eyebrow. "You've got guts, I'll give you that."

So why did they disappear whenever she came across Kevrina's gang?

Granted, she was still nervous about this. And getting on a horse she knew almost nothing about might not have been that smart, but so far Toperaz had proven to be nice enough on the ground. She hoped that his good temperament would carry over to when she was up in the saddle.

Grabbing the pommel, she put one foot in the stirrup and swung the other over the horse's back, settling herself in the large saddle. The stallion shifted under her, pawing the ground, and pulling on the reins, just like Neil whenever he really wanted to go.

"Think he's faster than Tomahawk?" she asked.

Leo grinned. "I dunno. Tommy's pretty fast." He patted his horse's neck. Then he froze. "Someone's coming up the stable path. Let's hoof it!"

Neither horse needed any urging: both took off in an instant. Tomahawk was quick on his feet; he drew ahead of the larger horse as they disappeared into the woods. But Toperaz stretched out his stride, and within a few minutes he started to overtake him.

Eiryenne sat in the saddle, the reins flapping about in the wind. She let them stay long; Toperaz was a powerful, strong-willed horse, and in truth she couldn't have held him back if she'd wanted to. The draft horse had a smooth, rocking gait; his gallop was comfortable to sit, too.

Their horses galloped between the tree trunks, following the winding forest path. Dappled light glanced off their coats as they ran beneath a canopy of lush green leaves and twisting branches.

Something rustled in the bushes in front of them, and Toperaz made a sudden detour, weaving between the trees and leaping over logs. There was a large, fallen tree that they were approaching rapidly, its bark speckled with green moss. Eiryenne started to pull on the reins, but the horse ignored her. He cleared the tree easily, leaping over it to land with a splash in a shallow pool on the other side. Leo followed, his horse clipping the edge of the log with a hind hoof.

They tore through an open field, neck to neck by now, before finding the trail again and galloping on. They followed the track, circling the outer perimeter of the camp and occasionally coming across mounted patrols. Eiryenne hoped they were going too fast and were too far away for the others to make out which horse she rode.

Finally, their horses started to tire and slowed to a canter. His energy spent, Toperaz dipped his head and accepted the rein pressure, slowing down. They stopped in a wooded clearing.

Eiryenne looked around. "I haven't been to this part of the trails before."

Leo laughed. "I don't think this *is* part of the trails. We went off course when Toperaz spooked."

"So where exactly are we?" She stood in the stirrups, looking around. There was a lake in front of them, its glassy surface sparkling under shafts of sunlight. She didn't remember a lake near the camp.

"No idea," Leo looked around. Then he shrugged. "Probably near the north boundary. Well, somewhere near there. We couldn't have gone that far."

Eiryenne's horse snorted and walked over to the lake, dipping his head, and taking a long drink.

"Y'know," Leo looked thoughtful, "maybe it was the right thing to do, taking him out. At least no one will look for him here." He paused, his mind already ten steps ahead of his mouth. "I've been thinking. We've got magic lessons. And we've got mounted archery lessons. But we don't have mounted magic lessons. I wonder why? It can't be that hard." He chattered on. Then he raised his hand and pointed at a rock on the ground. "*Horali santiagroyo daravaa!*" Yellow light rose from his fingers and pooled around the rock. It raised the boulder off the ground then cracked it in midair. The pieces made their way halfway to the lake before dropping suddenly.

"Lost my concentration," Leo said. "Tommy spooked." He panted. "Gotta give me some credit, though, right?"

Eiryenne smiled. "I don't think he's used to magic. Maybe that's why we don't practice magic from horseback—we don't have any horses trained to be around it."

"Well, they're certainly not going to get any more used to it if we just sit around. *Toarovati hano!*"

This time two leaves began to wrap themselves around a strand of grass and grow at the same time. As before, Leo lost his focus when his horse moved.

"Let me try. Maybe Toperaz is used to it—I mean, Molekk's a mage after all. *Horali!*" The rock in front of her barely got off the ground before Toperaz spooked.

"Yeah, a mage who never rode his horse," Leo said.

Noting how they horses seemed to be spooking just as much at the shouted incantation as they were at the light, Eiryenne sent out a plume of her purple blue magic with a silent thought, curling it around a tree trunk and forming a barrier. Then, deciding to try something new, she combined it with a quiet incantation. "*Destyrevan.*" It was a curious sensation as the unbridled energy of her unspoken spell was changed and channelled through that mental gate and into the new spell that she envisioned. The tree began to turn blue. Toperaz didn't spook as badly this time.

Leo got off his horse and tried to cast a spell beside Tomahawk, but his horse still pulled away. He sighed.

"It takes some training for this kind for thing, I'd imagine," she said. "I remember how Chief would spook at Danzi's fire and true form, and Neil had no idea what to do during a fight except run away. But they were farm horses, trail horses. These guys should at least be trained for battle. I guess magic is one step further, though."

"Yeah, from what I've seen, most horses will spook at things like minotaurs and Lianos if they're not used to it," Leo said.

Motion in the trees behind Leo caught Eiryenne's eye. Something big was behind that oak tree. But when she moved her gaze toward it, the shape flickered and changed. She could now make out the figure of Lianos standing in the shadows of the trees. He saw her looking and put a finger to his lips.

"Have you seen Lianos's true form?" Eiryenne asked. "I keep on missing it."

The elf boy nodded. "Yeah. It's pretty cool."

Lianos moved forward silently. The dappled light flashed off his draconic eyes and the silver buttons of his shirt. He might not have had his brother's commanding presence, but there was still an aura of underlying power about him; he was a dragon, and that was never to be taken lightly. His motions were fluid and light, but Eiryenne recognized the stalk. Lianos was hunting.

"Does he have fire magic like Danzi, too?" she continued.

"Yup. Blue fire, though. I've seen him casting spells a couple of times. It's amazing. Lianos is pretty cool," he paused. "Not as impressive as Danzi, though."

Lianos jumped forward and grabbed Leo from behind in a headlock.

"Ahh!" Leo jumped, startled.

"Not as impressive, eh?" Lianos said, grinning. Eiryenne had a quick flashback to him breaking Rol's neck when they first met. But then both elf and dragon mage began to laugh, and she relaxed.

"All right," Leo said. "You got me. Why do I *never* hear you coming?" He tapped his pointed ears in mock frustration.

"Good for keeping you on your toes. I might not be as infamous as my brother, but I'm usually a good deal quieter." Lianos loosened his mock headlock and stood back. "You've got a point; I don't have Danzi's reputation. Which, for the record, might be a good thing." He turned to look at Eiryenne, nodding at Toperaz. "You've taken a page from his book, it appears."

"Er," she looked sheepish. "Will you tell?"

Lianos shrugged. "I won't go out of my way to report it, no. But that explains why you are all the way out here. These are the west boundary woods, not the part we let you all ride in."

"We kind of went off course a little," Leo said. He mounted his horse again, looking thoughtful. "Hey, Lianos, since you're going to have to show us the way back and everything, I was thinking, is a dragon faster than a horse?"

There was a twinkle in the dragon mage's eye. "Only one way to find out."

Blinding white-blue flames surrounded his silhouette, and in the blink of an eye he shifted to his dragon shape.

Both horses drew back. Tomahawk reared.

Eiryenne couldn't tear her eyes away.

An elegant blue dragon stood in Lianos's place. His general shape was the same as Danzi's, but his build was more slender. He had the rectangular-shaped jaws and lion-like body, but on a different scale. Though he still towered over both the riders, Eiryenne thought he might have been a bit smaller than his brother. The dragon's scales gleamed like a multitude of flat sapphires, sparkling with different shades of blue. His head was crowned with horns of gleaming silver, matching the silver spines that ran along his back. The ridges above his eyes, too, were tipped with silver. The flat rows of belly scales that started under his neck were a soft, crystal-like light blue. Two neatly folded blue wings hung from his shoulders.

He stepped out from beneath the trees and without another word took off across the clearing. Eiryenne and Leo reined in their horses and urged them to follow. They ran with the dragon through the woods until the lake was well behind, first following a path, then cutting off the trail and through the brush.

While each of the horses had a distinct four-beat gallop angled to one lead or another, Lianos's movement was different. The dragon bounded forward, first striking the ground with his hind legs and propelling himself onward, then touching down with both front paws at the same time in a sort of sweeping motion. Despite the speed, the blue dragon's motions appeared fluid and effortless but also calculated; he seemed to place each step with great care in order to snag a minimal amount of debris. His wings were tucked in tightly at his sides, and he weaved occasionally to avoid catching them on branches.

Leo smacked Tomahawk on the rump, and the horse lengthened his stride, but he still couldn't catch the dragon. Eiryenne had lost interest in the race and let Toperaz run at whatever speed he chose. Her horse seemed content to watch from the back at first, but as they all came over a log, the jump seemed to give him second wind and he took off at a full gallop again. Tomahawk, on the other hand, looked disheartened at being made to jump things when he didn't want to and follow things he didn't like. He began to slow. Then Toperaz overtook him, and he sped up again. Even if he was content losing to a dragon, it was clear he didn't want to lose to another horse again.

There was another log up ahead. Lianos floated over it without missing a stride. He seemed to hang in the air for a second, pulling all the sunlight in the woods toward him until it settled amidst the sapphire blue of his scales and made them gleam and spark. Eiryenne followed him, marvelling at how the blue dragon almost seemed to glide on his very elevated, lofty gait. It looked like it would be lovely to ride.

Then they jumped onto a trail again, and soon Eiryenne could see the outlines of the stables and fences in the distance. They were back.

"Gonna take him to mounted archery practice?" Leo asked, gesturing to Toperaz.

"No," she said, still panting slightly after the gallop. "I think that would be a little too much."

Lianos left them soon after, but Leo and Eiryenne bumped into him again after they put their horses away.

"Well, from what I saw, you two look like you could both use some practice with nonverbal magic," he said.

So, another class was added to Eiryenne's camp timetable. Not that she really minded; lessons with Lianos were challenging but rewarding, and she knew that she needed the practice. So far, she'd concentrated only on the verbal magic Riard was teaching her; her instinctual magic skills were rusty, as she quickly found out during their first lesson. Something else that she lacked was the ability to really push herself, because unlike Danzi, Lianos was not going to do that for her. His methods were simple and straightforward. He gave out the instructions, but it was up to his students to apply them; there was no surprise or hidden danger if they failed. He'd simply shrug and ask her to try again, or after enough tries, switch to something else.

One day Kevrina and Hilla approached, snidely asking to join the lesson. Eiryenne was confident that he'd refuse, but to her surprise Lianos politely accepted and resumed their barrier-enchantment practice without further ado. When they tried to enchant Eiryenne's shirt and his own vest, however, he cut off their spells in a flash of blue fire. He made it clear that he'd tolerate no tomfoolery in his lessons. The other girls were allowed in if they behaved. But since that obviously wasn't their goal, they soon left.

Healing was one thing that Lianos didn't teach. He reiterated what Danzi said: a dragon mage wasn't the best person to teach healing.

From then on, however, Eiryenne's training now covered all bases. Yolen had started teaching her to heal as well as shoot; Riard continued the communal verbal magic, lessons as well as tutoring her in writing; Stroman taught the physical side of combat, and Lianos filled in whatever was missing.

There was only one obstacle now.

Kevrina.

And Danzi was right. It was time to take matters into her own hands.

7 ~ Plans and Revelations

"Mind if I browse?" Eiryenne asked.

"Not at all," said Riard. He went on about how it was nice to see youth take interest in books and how it would serve them well if more did.

Eiryenne went up to the bookshelf and looked through the stacks of dusty volumes. During the past few weeks, she'd learned that if one looked hard enough, almost anything could be found in Riard's private library.

Do your research, Danzi had said. *Get to know their tactics.*

She found the book she was looking for, having spotted it the previous day. *All about Fabric Enchantments and Counter-Spells.* Now she hopefully knew enough Elvish to read it. Eiryenne also took a copy of *A Study of Pseudopoisons, Magic and Culture of the Kive Peoples,* and *A Guide to Common Magical Traps.*

She read them in between lessons and during evenings in her hidden cabin, reading by candlelight about ways to predict, prevent, and stop fabric enchantments, as well as researching potential Kive spells that she might have to watch out for from Hilla.

Eiryenne practiced the spell that would repel a fabric enchantment, weaving the magic into her memory so that it could be there at a moment's notice. Because that was all she'd get.

Get to know their tactics. Exploit them.

The girls kept her on her toes during magic lessons. But she was getting quicker at dodging spells and putting up barriers under pressure. Kevrina and Hilla didn't know it, but they were making Eiryenne a stronger mage through all their pestering. And she was getting used to predicting the swirl of pinkish light that meant Kevrina was about to enchant something. Thanks to the book, she knew that the swirling light was her magic being shaped by a physical or mental incantation, evolving into the spell that would be cast. There was a brief lull before the spell solidified and met the fabric, where, in theory, a magical pull in the opposite direction would cause a breakdown.

The gang usually left her alone during combat practice unless they'd cooked up something particularly nasty. This time, Eiryenne looked on with her mage vision as a swirl of Kevrina's pink light combined with Hilla's purple. The Kive magic would be harder to get around. It was quicker and more stable, cutting Eiryenne's window of opportunity in half.

Eiryenne gripped the sword in her hand as she forged the spell she needed in her mind. Then, with a mental flick, she sent her small turquoise spear of light straight into the vortex of pink and purple. It didn't have to be strong, just accurate. She anchored it to the bottom, imagining it latching on to the other spell with a dragon's jaws. Then, like the fiery hurricane Danzi cast against the ice mage, Eiryenne spread out her magic and spun it in the opposite direction.

The effect was instantaneous. The other girls' spell fell apart and smashed into the ground around them instead of the pile of tunics next to Eiryenne, where they'd been aiming. The earth bubbled like lava, and they sank into it up to their waists.

Whether that was supposed to happen or if it was a side-effect of her bringing dragon magic into her thoughts, Eiryenne didn't know.

She just quietly stepped into the shadows while someone ran for a mage.

Find an advantage. Press it.

While Riard was still extracting the girls from the earth, Eiryenne went to their cabin. This time she was ready for the spray of corrosive liquid that shot into her face as she opened the door. The distinctive acrid odour belonged to Oilder oil, something she'd found in the magical traps book and confirmed by one of the labelled vials in Riard's study. Also from his study, she'd brought a flask of Toperal potion. She raised it out in front of her with her magic, holding it in a thin film across her barrier. The Oilder oil sputtered and turned to water, harmlessly falling to the floor.

She closed the door and walked over to Kevrina's bunk. There were letters in Elvish scrawled across her bed, glowing pink.

Eiryenne took a page out of her pocket that she'd copied from one of the books and compared the symbols until she found a match.

Heat-sensitive barrier spell.

Her page offered a counter-spell; it was one of several that she'd rehearsed. Squinting at the letters, she called on her magic and spoke the incantation.

"*Molerava kli,*" she muttered. Her magic flowed around the symbols and extinguished them.

She stuffed the paper back into her pocket and climbed up the ladder to the pink bed and the trunk at its foot. There was another trap here, but her sheet served her well, and soon it too was neutralized.

Finally, she lifted the corner of the trunk. Beneath a bunch of extra clothes, she found her Bremian sword, dagger, and pack. She buckled them onto her belt on the spot.

Eiryenne hurried out, feeling shaky despite herself. But she wouldn't give in to the panic again. Nor would she be caught.

She was wrong. Kevrina and Hilla were furious, and they found her walking to her magic lesson with Lianos. She almost didn't see the flash of magic until it was too late. Then the ground disappeared beneath her left foot. She jumped to the side and rolled out of the way as a torrent of pink and purple light tore through the space where she had been standing just a second before.

Behind her, she saw the two mage girls, their expressions murderous.

Eiryenne drew her Bremian sword. It felt familiar in her grip, and its comforting weight calmed her frantic heart. She coated it with spells of cutting and slicing and deflecting before throwing up a barrier to block their next attack. But combined, the girls were decidedly more powerful than her.

She struck down the next enchantment when she saw it coming, but this time the ground around her foes stayed stable; Hilla caught the magic and redirected it into a tangle of light that caught Eiryenne's boots and shrank them until the blood supply to her feet was cut off. Eiryenne managed to take a few more steps before she fell. She slapped the leather with the flat of her blade and the spell released.

Eiryenne knew she was outmatched. There were no other mages in sight. She'd be at their mercy again.

Well, perhaps not.

She ran forward, their spells glancing off her weakening barrier. Then she was directly between them, but by now her barrier had taken so much punishment that it drained the last of her magic. She lowered it and ducked. Their shafts of light collided and hit one another. One of Hilla's cutting spells went to Kevrina instead, almost cutting across her windpipe. But Eiryenne redirected it at the last second. She wanted them incapacitated, not dead.

Taking advantage of the confusion, Eiryenne grabbed hold of their magic with her mind and twisted it into a confusing tangle, making their spells rebound off each other.

It worked for about five seconds.

Before Eiryenne could even get to her feet, Hilla abandoned her spells and jumped forward with her knife. Too late did the other girl realize she'd dropped her sword amongst all the magical fuss.

A figure emerged from the shadows.

"Is there a problem?" Lianos asked mildly.

Grudgingly, the girls backed off and headed away.

The dragon mage helped Eiryenne to her feet. "Someone's been doing their homework," he said quietly. With a jolt, Eiryenne realized he'd been watching them the whole time. "Good job."

"Thanks, but I got too caught up in the magic," she muttered, still panting. "Forgot about my sword. I didn't think they'd actually—"

"The Kive are quite fond of their knives," he said. "They're more bloodthirsty than appearances may lead you to believe. It's something you should remember next time."

"Yeah, I–oww!" A sudden pain in her left arm made her look down. She rolled up her sleeve. One of Kevrina's spells must have hit her, because her skin was tinted with pink light. It began to crawl and move like the fabrics she enchanted, threatening to peel itself right off her bones. She tried to smooth it out with her fingers, but the effect just passed to them as well.

Then there was a light touch on her arm and a soft blue glow. Lianos quickly swept his hand down her forearm, and her skin settled back into place, Kevrina's pink magic replaced by the familiar tingling feeling of dragonfire.

"Haven't seen that one before," he said. "And that's saying something."

Eiryenne ran her fingers down her arm, double-checking the firmness of her skin. "Thank you," she said. Then she hesitated. "Why are you being nice to me? Is it because of Danzi?"

Lianos looked amused. "I just think you're a good person. And," he looked pensive, "you remind me of-of someone I used to know when I was your age. He was a lot like you. Problems with confidence, bullies, etcetera. Then he began to take control, just like you're doing now. So, I know it's not an easy thing, and I'm glad that you're doing it." He paused "Because you can't live in fear."

"Your friend, where is he now?"

Leo came around the corner just then. "Well, I'm ready to start," he announced. "What'll we be doing today?"

Eiryenne was out of magic, but a little extra theory never hurt.

Strengthen your own weaknesses. Train.

"Well, Lianos," she began, "what if, in theory, someone was trying a rebound enchantment. What could you improve on, as a mage, to prevent that sort of thing from happening?"

A smile tugged at the dragon mage's lips. "Well, in theory…"

***

"Your magic doesn't really look like a Kive's," Eiryenne said, watching Riard's green light stack pages onto a high shelf. "Not an elf, either. And something tells me you're not human. What's your heritage, if you don't mind me asking?"

"Oh, I'm a mix of pretty much everything—elf, Druid, human, et cetera," Riard said, looking amused. "You can see this reflected in my magic if you look closely. I'm a multipurpose mage, a generalist who specializes in no one thing but can do a bit of many." He paused. "Not all, though. For example, Druids are earth mages and grow stuff, but I can't grow a thing to save my life." He chuckled. Then he pointed to a paragraph on the page and got up. "Read through that. I have some Council paperwork to go sort out. I'll be back in about ten minutes." He walked out the door then popped his head back inside. "Oh, and try to find that inkwell and that manuscript we were working through, will you? It got lost somewhere in the clutter of my study." Then he headed off.

Eiryenne walked over to his desk. A couple of wayward spells had wreaked havoc on his occasionally organized papers. Finding anything here would be hard today.

She'd gone through a couple of boring manuscripts when a partly open drawer at the bottom of the desk caught her eye. She hadn't noticed it before. Riard must have shut it in a hurry, and the automatic lock spell hadn't taken.

Eiryenne bent down and reached in. Her fingers found themselves feeling the corners of some rolled-up scrolls and tapestries. She opened the first one. It was another landscape, painted with wild, impressionistic strokes on a strange kind of crumbly paper. There was a caption in the corner. "Glades of northern Remfuria." Below it was a signature—*Riard Ershke.*

She looked up at the landscape painting that hung on the wall. Had he done that one as well? If he did, then obviously his style had changed drastically over the years. Or maybe it hadn't changed that quickly, if, like Danzi, Riard was a lot older than he looked.

Eiryenne carefully moved the old painting out of the way. Next was a tapestry. It showed a group of warriors on the battlefield, hands raised in victory. There was the lion again. He looked to be the leader. If she wasn't mistaken, that's who Danzi was accused of killing. Maybe that's why everyone was mad at him.

But somehow, she thought it ran deeper than that.

The tapestry after that was similar. At the centre of the image was a man dressed in gold armour. But next to him was another man dressed in bronze-coloured armour with red chain mail. There was no mistaking that ruby-hilted broadsword or pointed blonde beard.

Danzi.

Beside Danzi was a woman that Eiryenne didn't recognize, dressed in sleek powder blue and white armour, with long, pale hair and a sword glowing pure white.

The girl paused, staring at the stranger's face. On second thought, perhaps she *had* seen her somewhere before. But for the life of her, Eiryenne couldn't remember where.

Next to the woman was an elf with long, light hair and a crossbow, wearing armour patterned with leaves. It was Leo's dad, Yolen. Eiryenne then spotted another familiar face at the end of the image — Riard, with green armour over his robes and a glowing staff in hand.

There was an inscription in Elvish on the bottom, but it was an older, different dialect from the one she'd learned, and Eiryenne could only make out the names and judge the rest to be the description of some kind of historic battle.

She turned to the next tapestry. The top was folded over, and while she set to carefully straightening the aged fabric, Eiryenne observed the visible portion of the bottom. There were more soldiers, some of the same ones from the other tapestry — she recognized Riard and Yolen. Lianos was also there, though Danzi, the woman in blue, and the man in gold were absent. This time, however, the scale was much larger. The tapestry showed an army in mid-charge across a field. Among men and elves, she saw, to her surprise, Dyre wolves. Griffins, pegasi, and winged cats flew above them. And there, beside the elves, were unicorns. Not black or twisted like Tairung, but proper unicorns like the one in Danzi's dream, dazzling white with iridescent, pearly horns.

The top of the tapestry was caught on something. While she continued to work it with her fingers, Eiryenne peered down at the caption. It was in that weird form of Elvish again.

Gritting her teeth, she tried to piece together the translation from the little she knew.

Battle of Olungery. That wasn't too hard. Next was something about the Resistance army. A few of the noted officers. And ... *Tarangil Danzellius.*

Again, something to do with Danzi. She recognized the dragon mage's full name, but the word preceding it eluded her. What she needed was an Elvish-Common dictionary. She wondered whether Riard had one somewhere.

Then the tapestry gave, and the top portion flipped open onto her lap.

It showed a magnificent, brilliantly coloured red dragon in full flight above the army. His jaws were parted in a roar, and fire leaped from his claws. He wasn't attacking the army, though, just flying above it.

If Danzi was considered an enemy of the Council, Eiryenne could see why Riard kept these well locked up.

Who was he, though? Who was Danzi before he became the wandering rogue? That's clearly not who he was in these images.

The truth was close; she could sense it. It was right under her nose. Something she was missing. Something to do with these old, hidden tapestries.

She came across the red dragon again a few tapestries in. He was shown flying next to the golden lion, who had wings in this image. Golenhar, that was his name. The founder. The first leader of the Resistance.

And in the inscription, that same word again, before both their names.

Tarangil Golenhar. Tarangil Danzellius.

That was when it clicked.

Eiryenne's jaw dropped.

Tarangil was Elvish for *Leader.*

Just then, Riard walked back in. He stopped dead when he saw the tapestry in her hands.

Eiryenne gasped, still trying to process what she'd read. "Danzi was the *leader*?"

The mage sighed. "Yes. Yes, he was."

"But what happened?"

Riard sighed. "A lot."

Grehar's furious face slid into her thoughts. "Did he really kill Golenhar? Is that what it was?"

Riard shook his head. "No. Golenhar was slain by Varcroft's general. I and anyone else who was there on that day can attest to that. Of course, some will choose to support the rumours but that is all they are: rumours." He paused. "Golenhar recommended Danzi as his successor, and the Council came to the same decision. Danzi's reign started out superbly and ended in disaster. His triumphs were great. But so were his mistakes."

Eiryenne listened, rapt with attention. Suddenly there was far more to the lone rebel, the mysterious outcast than she ever thought.

"He conquered more territory than Golenhar and Hurraine put together; under his command, we drove the Empire back, bit by bit, battle by battle. Danzi was an experienced military leader, as well as a brilliant tactician; and it showed. We were gaining ground like never before. Morale was high in those days." Riard looked pensive. "We almost, some of us almost dared to hope that this war was finally coming to an end. And then," he sighed, "the downfall. After months of being virtually unbeaten, Danzi made a fatal error at the Battle of Kyrahgrun, and the Resistance lost over half its army. We were decimated." He rubbed his forehead, his expression grim. "It only got worse from there. Danzi lost his motivation. A string of more losses followed as he struggled to escape with what was left of our army. And when we did finally get out of that hellhole, the Council kicked him out. The decision was unanimous. Danzi was no longer deemed fit to command the Resistance."

A figure had appeared in the doorway, listening to their conversation. It was Lianos. "I remember that," he said heavily. "Danzi knew it was coming. But he didn't take the news very well."

"They said he ran," Eiryenne mumbled. "They said he ran away."

Riard sighed again. "He couldn't stand to remain here with his command taken from him. So he left. And he searched high and low to find the one that he blamed for his downfall … the black pegasus, Blackthorn."

Goosebumps formed on Eiryenne's skin as she remembered the raw, bloody hatred with which Danzi had turned upon the pegasus. "What did Blackthorn do?"

"He was a spy," Riard said. "No one knows how long he had been passing information to the other side before he finally fled. But we do know that he'd leaked some very crucial details to the Empire, giving them a definite advantage. Add to that the fact that he killed Danzi's best friend at Kyrahgrun. Well, you can imagine how much the dragon wants to kill him."

Eiryenne shook her head. No wonder there was so much controversy surrounding Danzi. But if he was innocent of some of his accusations, what about the pegasus? "So is Blackthorn really to blame for all that Danzi says he is?" she asked.

Riard shrugged. "There is no doubt that he contributed to what happened at Kyrahgrun and caused Freya's death. However, the extent of what he shared remains unknown. In hard times, people like to have some one person to point their finger at. In a way, Blackthorn has become Danzi's scapegoat, in the same way that Danzi has become the Resistance's."

"We met Blackthorn in the Empire," Eiryenne said quietly. The two men raised their eyebrows. "Danzi went crazy."

Lianos nodded. "I'm not surprised. Even though he started to get a handle on his temper after he became the Resistance leader, nowadays Blackthorn will make him snap on sight."

Eiryenne blinked. "Danzi used to be even *more* explosive? Good thing I didn't know him then."

Lianos's face darkened. "Yes, a very good thing."

"Anyway, after his leadership was taken from him, Danzi left the Resistance on the hunt for Blackthorn," continued Riard. "After the trail ran cold, he began working with us again, indirectly, of course. He refused to submit to Hurraine's rule, and most of our warriors hated him anyway. But he's still completed some important missions during his years as a rogue. He wasn't afraid to go deep inside the Empire by himself, and a dragon could go places that most other warriors couldn't. Years went by. We knew that he was still working for the Resistance in his own roundabout way, but even I never expected him to fly into this camp again."

They were all silent for a moment, each lost in their own thoughts. Then Eiryenne thought of a new question. "Wait, so if Danzi didn't kill Golenhar, and his downfall was a combination of factors, why is everybody still blaming him for pretty much everything?" she asked.

"Like I said, in times of crisis, people like to have someone to blame," Riard said. "Spies like Blackthorn, circumstances, details, all of that can fade from people's minds. What stands out is the leader who let his people down and then abandoned them. That fact was ingrained in the minds of everyone who survived Kyrahgrun and has been retold to newer recruits and children. They started to twist the truth to suit their anger. And in their frustration, they began pinning other things on Danzi as well. Everything from Golenhar's death to their subsequent struggles became his fault. Danzi's successor, Hurraine, encouraged this. By having everyone so focused on hating Danzi, she would appear a better leader. Even if her success never came close to what the other two leaders actually achieved, next to this bad caricature of Danzi, she would look good."

"There remains a small circle of people," Lianos said, "who still support Danzi. These include Riard and myself, as well as Yolen, who I believe you met earlier. There are others, as well. A valiant group of warriors who had seen through Hurraine's deceptions and knew that she would not be the one to lead them to their ultimate victory. Most, if not all of us are at the camp right now, for one reason or another. I took the long route back to camp when I heard about the call to arms."

"We knew that Hurraine was walking into a trap," Riard said. "But she wouldn't listen to us. She heard about the Necklace and assumed that the Emperor would send his army after it, leaving the capital exposed to attack."

"We thought that was unlikely at best. And what Hurraine didn't know about was the war in the north and that the Emperor had already mobilized his troops with no intention of wasting an entire army on you two," Lianos added. "We only found that out when Danzi told us. He gets around farther in the Empire than most of our other agents do. But I won't be surprised if they blame him when Hurraine's army is defeated."

"I'll say something," Riard said. "Danzi's had his fair share of trouble, but he owns up to his mistakes, and it's not fair to him to continue to blame him for everything."

"I agree, but do you really think they'll listen to us?" said Lianos. "I'm his brother; you had your life saved by him."

"He saved your life?" Eiryenne asked.

Riard nodded. "I almost died at Kyrahgrun," he said quietly. "It was … it was a mess. We had no chance to set up a healing tent during the battle; everyone was fighting, from the healers to the children. I took a pike to the torso mid-battle. It was only after the fighting was over and done with that they had a chance to take it out and try to fix me. I thought it was all over for me … then I awakened to the most intense, searing pain in my chest. And there was Danzi, his armour bent and bloodied, and his hand on my wound, sealing it together." He looked thoughtful. "People say I'm biased because of that. I tell them, if I wasn't already his friend, he wouldn't have saved me, now would he?"

Eiryenne nodded, still trying to process it all.

Danzi Daggoras, the great fallen leader. She could barely wrap her head around it. But beneath her disbelief, she realized how everything made sense now. People were bitter because they thought he'd abandoned them. His losses had only been reinforced and exaggerated by the next leader. Everyone new was taught that he was a traitor. Only a few of his old war buddies were still faithful to him, for one reason or another. Yolen was one of them; it was no wonder he'd raised his son on tales of Danzi's triumphs. That was why Leo alone among the young elves idolized him. And from the snatches of Elvish she'd heard from his aunt and uncle, it was clear that they, on the other hand, were no fans of the red dragon.

"And the rest of those creatures?" She recognized the elves and minotaurs, but the tapestry also showed winged lions and unicorns, which she'd yet to see in the camp. "We really had *unicorns?*"

"In the beginning, yes. Then came Danzi's downfall, and we started to lose them, one by one the unicorns left after Kyrahgrun. They suffered enormous casualties there, as well as the scandal … the winged lions left shortly after. As for the Dyre wolves, we only had a handful of them to start with. Most were killed or fled."

After leaving Riard's cabin, Eiryenne wandered over to the stables, still deep in thought. She still had trouble picturing the moody dragon leading an army. But maybe he wasn't so moody back then. Maybe the reason he was so dark and distant now was because of what had happened. It couldn't have all been his fault. There was the spy to consider, after all. Who knew what really happened on the battlefield that day?

Either way, it was clear that Danzi never got over it.

Neither had most of the people they'd met.

And they wouldn't. Not while they were still brooding over it, still bathing in their hatred.

To snap them all out of it would take something new. Something big.

8 ~ War Games Gone Awry

The rest of Eiryenne's summer at the camp sped by. Her days were occupied with training, fending off bullies, and riding. There were also the tournaments, voluntary competitions between the kids in a certain field. She had little interest in the sword tournaments; it was the archery competitions that caught her eye. Her accuracy improved with practice until she was near the top of the human pack, but she had miles to go before she could catch the elves' speed.

Over months of formal training and confrontations with Kevrina, her magic skills continued to improve and grow. And as she spent most of her free time in the saddle galloping over the scenic trails with Leo, Tina, and Lianos, her riding abilities also improved, and she began to expand her range of mounts up to more challenging ones. And though her heart was still in her mouth every time she approached Toperaz's paddock, she continued to take him out behind Molekk's back because it was the right thing to do.

Her fourteenth birthday came and went as May rolled by. Leo let her keep the bow she borrowed as a present. His attitude toward her was improving. Now he no longer bombarded her with questions about the past; he seemed to enjoy spending time with her for who she was, not what she'd done.

No matter the weather, she'd still start each morning with Danzi's warm-up exercises, sometimes joined by Tina and Leo. Grindt tried them out one time as well, but he just couldn't bend his arms all the way behind his back. Eiryenne felt sorry for him; Grindt jogged for hours every day, trained as hard as anyone, but he still couldn't shed those pounds or the remarks that followed them.

Lessons with Lianos were always interesting, and they grew ever more complex as June turned to July and August was upon them. He worked her and Leo hard, having them combine various kinds of magic and teaching them new spells by the day. He'd also do some knifework every now and again, if he felt that Stroman had left too much out in a particular day.

Eiryenne's clashes with Kevrina grew more intense, but she found she was less nervous each time and had to use the calming herbs less frequently. Sometimes she even found herself telling the older girls off for bothering kids like Larkden. It felt good, she found. Even though it was still scary.

Then, in mid-August, the adults decided to hold war games. The kids would be split into teams and set against each other in the north woods, a normally out-of-bounds section of the forest, with some dangerous creatures also released there for good measure. There were four defending teams and three attacking ones; the defenders had to prevent their coloured sticks from being stolen, while the attacking teams had to try and take as many as they could — one from each defending team.

As Eiryenne suspected, Kevrina and Tukse picked the oldest and strongest mages and warriors for their teams. In the end, Eiryenne was assigned to a team with Leo, Grindt, and Larkden. To her surprise, Taymel joined the team as well.

She didn't look happy about it.

"They're mad," she said to Eiryenne. "They're mad that I insulted their embroidery yesterday. They wouldn't let me on their team."

Eiryenne raised her eyebrows. "You, insulting their embroidery? That's a new one." Kevrina might have been a jerk, but even Eiryenne could see she was great with a needle and thread.

"Their embroidery was bad, honestly," Taymel said. She paused, looking around. "It's because Kevrina got into trouble over that silly elf amulet. Y'know," she looked at the ground, "the one she got from you."

"The one she *stole* from me. But it wasn't mine. I borrowed it from Danzi. Anyway, what happened?"

"Well, it turns out that it was actually some kind of ancient, sacred elven artefact and it was heresy to even come close to it. All the elves ganged up on her and yelled at her the whole evening. I'm surprised you didn't hear. It was a disaster. She was in so much trouble with the adults. And then some of the kids put a spell on her embroidery needles."

"Serves her right." Eiryenne shrugged. After everything she'd endured from the other girl, she had little sympathy for her. Justice had come at last.

"You're lucky they didn't see it on *you*."

"All right," Riard called from where he stood in the centre of the arena. "These are your teams. Now pick your team colours."

Tukse went with green, Kevrina with purple, and the other attacking team with blue. The defending teams went with yellow, black, and orange.

Then Riard turned to the last team. "Well?"

"Umm ...." Leo looked unsure. He elbowed Eiryenne. "The good ones are already taken. You don't want to be Team Pink now, do you?"

"I got it," she said. She turned to Riard. "Red. We'll be the Red Team."

Riard waved his hands over the bare, sharpened sticks that were on the ground in front of him. Three of each turned each of the four defending team's colours. Then he raised his staff, and the sticks flew out to drop at the corresponding team's feet.

Eiryenne picked up their red sticks. The top of each had a coloured band of green, purple, or blue, corresponding to each of the attacking teams.

"Take your sticks, defending teams," Riard called out. "You have fifteen minutes before I release the attackers. They will then try to get one stick from each of the defending teams. The team with the most sticks on either side in two hours wins. Go!"

They all took off at a sprint, but Eiryenne's team soon had to slow down to accommodate Grindt's slow trot. She could see that he was trying — he simply couldn't move his stubby legs any faster. But that didn't stop the others from throwing him dirty looks.

Leo took the lead, taking them up a path through the woods that went to a pond. Eiryenne turned back every now and again, sweeping away their tracks with a whoosh of magic. She suggested that they follow the perimeter and head for the west end of the woods; people weren't likely to go there since they didn't know the area. But she and Leo had ridden through it once by accident.

They kept going even when the horn signalling the hunters' release went off fifteen minutes later. In about half an hour, they holed up in a grassy hollow and settled down to wait it out.

"That ditch looks good," Leo said.

"Okay." Eiryenne nodded. "Let's put some spells on it then. The rest of you can keep a lookout."

They positioned their three sticks deep in the rocky ditch. Eiryenne and Leo took turns covering it in barriers and protective spells that they could activate at any sign of trouble — so that they wouldn't have to drain their magic unnecessarily.

"Now, shouldn't we have a battle plan?" Eiryenne said.

Leo shrugged and took out his bow. "If someone comes, shoot them."

Eiryenne took hers out, too, making sure there were arrows in her quiver within easy reach. The sword she'd save for later if it came to close-quarters combat.

Larkden sat down on a log. He looked grim. "We're doomed," he said. "We're gonna lose so badly, it'll be a new record."

"An attitude like that's already half the battle lost," Eiryenne said. "Look, why don't you climb that ridge and keep a lookout? If you see someone coming, make some kind of spell to send those pinecones raining over their heads. It'll be a good distraction."

"Whatever."

Eiryenne turned to Grindt, looking thoughtful. "Grindt, you're strong. You should stay by the ravine. There are a lot of big boulders here. Try throwing them at the attacking team."

"All right."

"And Taymel ..." She trailed off.

"Taymel can be the second lookout and our first line of defence after the ridge," Leo piped up. He looked at Eiryenne and mouthed the word *expendable*. She frowned.

Everyone took up their positions and began to wait. The minutes ticked by. Eiryenne's palms soon started to get sweaty. She shifted the bow in her grip. Kevrina would be coming soon, with a pack of her hand-picked wolves at her side. This time it would be full-out war.

Well, as much as fights between mages like them could be called war.

"Do the adults have war games, too?" she asked Leo.

"Nah," he replied. "They've got the real thing." Then his fingers flew to his lips as his sharp elven ears picked up the sounds of cracking twigs.

They barely had time to raise their bows before Tukse, Roben, Nur, and a young minotaur burst out of the brush.

Leo fired an arrow, but Tukse brushed it aside with a spell before paralyzing him with another. Roben and Nur rushed past Larkden, knocking him aside. Eiryenne fired at Tukse, judging him to be the biggest threat, but he dodged her arrow as if it were moving at a snail's pace. The younger elves easily avoided Taymel's sword and pushed her down the hill, tripping Eiryenne before ducking beneath Grindt's thrown boulders. The minotaur tackled her then launched itself at Grindt. Nur hit him with a spell for good measure, too. Tukse leaped over the struggling lot before scooping up the green-topped stick, and within seconds they'd gone, just as quickly as they arrived.

Leo groaned and sat up as the paralyzing spell wore off. "That went well," he said sarcastically.

"I told you we don't stand a chance," panted Larkden, spitting out a mouthful of the dirt he'd been pushed into. "This is pointless."

"Yeah, because you and Taymel are such dead weight," the elf grumbled.

Eiryenne picked up her bow. This was harder than she thought it would be. They were just so disorganized. Tukse's team seemed to know exactly what to do and how to work together, but the Red Team was falling apart at the seams.

It was hard enough when you just had to decide what you did in battle. Now, Eiryenne was struggling to coordinate a team of five. How Danzi had done it with an entire army was beyond her.

"We can do this," she said, trying to sound positive. "We just have to stay focused and work together."

This time not even Leo looked optimistic.

Despite their best efforts, the next attack by Team Blue went no better, and soon there was only one stick left in the ravine: the purple-topped one.

Eiryenne rubbed her bruises. If they could face off Kevrina's team, then personally she'd feel like it was a victory. She walked through the bushes, trying to find her teammates. The Blue Team's attack had left them bloodied and scattered in the woods. She found Grindt and left him at the ravine before heading back out to the trees. She knew she at least needed Leo at her side to have any chance against the Purple Team.

Unfortunately, she only found Larkden, huddled behind a tree stump. His sleeves were still smoking. He was muttering fervently under his breath, though the only result seemed to be that the grass around him waved and turned orange. He also ignored the girl and refused to budge.

"The song," he whispered. "The songs! They're inside my head." His eyes had gone listless, and he smacked the air in front of him in a rigid trance.

She'd seen his fits before, but not like this. Blue Team must have hit him in the head with something hard. But try as she might, she couldn't get through to him.

There was nothing she could do, so with a sigh, Eiryenne turned back. She'd gone far enough; Leo would have to find his way back on his own. She wasn't going to leave Grindt alone to face Kevrina and Hilla.

But when she returned to the ravine, all was quiet. Grindt was sitting on a log beside a big pile of rocks that he'd gathered, ready for throwing.

She was about to sit down next to him when the deep, resonating sound of a war horn blasted out across the woods.

"Is that it?" she said. "Are the games over?"

There was a frown on Grindt's chubby, mud-streaked face. "No," he said. "That was the alarm horn. That means the camp's under attack, for real!"

"Oh." Suddenly, losing a game seemed like such a trifling thing to be worried about. "What should we do?"

"I think we should just wait here," Grindt said. He sounded nervous. "We're far from the most direct routes to camp; hopefully, the intruders will pass by a long way from here. This is stuff for the adults to deal with."

"Right." Except that there weren't that many at camp.

They did have a dragon, though. Surely, short of an army, there was little that a dragon couldn't stop.

But what if it *was* an army? What if Varcroft had defeated Hurraine, as predicted, and followed her trail back to the camp?

Eiryenne shuddered.

An explosion in the distance made them both jump. There were shouts, too, but far off. At first Eiryenne nocked an arrow and stood at the ready, waiting for trouble to find them, but after a while it seemed as though Grindt was right. The commotion wasn't moving their way.

She sat down on the log next to him, keeping her bow in easy reach.

Leo and the others were still out there. She hoped they had the sense to hunker down and wait it out.

Somehow, she knew the elf wouldn't, though. He'd jump at the chance to participate in his first real battle.

Grindt was saying something, but his voice was slurred, and his eyes had rolled back into his head.

"Grindt?" she shook him. "Are you okay?"

"The singing," he murmured, going limp. "It's—"

"What singing?"

Suddenly the boy jerked upright again, blinking. "What happened?" he asked.

"You said something about singing," she frowned.

"I did?"

Rapidly approaching footfalls made her look up. She grabbed her bow and raised it just as a silvery grey creature burst out of the woods. It looked like a deer, with great, twisted antlers and long, spindly legs. Then its mouth opened down the length of its head, revealing four pairs of razor-sharp incisors.

Definitely not a deer, then.

It leaped over the ravine at great speed. An arrow whizzed through the air to graze its flank and embed itself in the tree behind it. Unwounded, the creature galloped off through the woods.

Another figure crashed through the undergrowth and hit the tree, sending another arrow toward the creature. Another miss.

It was Lianos, with a bow in his hand, running hard to catch the creature. But it was fast and manoeuvred better; he was never able to get a shot off quickly or accurately enough to hit it. Finally, he fell back, panting.

"Lianos, what's going on?" Eiryenne walked up to him, still holding her own bow. "Are we under attack? What was that thing?"

"That was a moon kirin," he said. "Very rare. Extremely dangerous and also very hard to catch. They can only be brought down by one of these." He tapped the arrows in his quiver. They had strange bronze heads that appeared to be glowing from the inside. "But I just can't — wait a minute." He looked from Eiryenne to her bow. "How good are you at mounted archery? Third place in the tournament, right?"

"Well, yeah, but I still don't get—"

"Take this." Without another word, Lianos passed her his quiver. Then he transformed. There was a row of spines running down the dragon's back that started at his neck and went all the way to the end of his tail. A patch of them around his shoulders started to glow then dissolved into blue fire and sank into his scales until there was a clear spot just big enough for a rider. "I hope you're in the mood for a hunt. Get on, girl. You're in for the ride of your life."

Hardly believing what she was doing, Eiryenne climbed up a half-fallen tree and clambered onto the dragon's back. She sat in the hollow he'd cleared of his spines, suddenly feeling very tall. The dragon was far taller than any horse, so she almost felt as if she was perched in a tree, so high was her new vantage point. The rock-hard scales beneath her legs shifted and softened until they had a softer, more leathery texture that was easier to grip.

"Ready?" Lianos's voice reverberated in the plates at her feet.

She nodded.

Lianos couldn't have seen the motion, but he must have felt it, because he turned and bounded off into the woods in pursuit of the moon kirin. At first Eiryenne was afraid that she'd impale herself on the spines on the dragon's neck, but she found that they were now relatively soft to the touch and pliable enough to hang on to.

The dragon flew up the path with long, smooth strides. His paws barely seemed to touch the ground as he moved, skimming the earth before bounding forward again. Then he took a turn into the bush, but his motion didn't slow. Unlike the horses Eiryenne had ridden that were limited by bad terrain or thick bushes, Lianos seemed to be able to move through anything. His claws gripped on rocky or unstable surfaces, and the branches didn't scratch his scales as he crashed through them.

At first Eiryenne clung on, slightly unnerved by the speed, but gradually she settled into the unfamiliar rhythm of the dragon's stride, not distinctly four-beat like a horse, but rather two, and so blurred together that it was like one single leap. And as Lianos jumped a log, landed on sheer rock, and took a hairpin turn without missing a step before ploughing uphill, she began to appreciate the sheer power of the animal beneath her.

If you rode a dragon, nothing and no one could stop you. Eiryenne's worries and concerns seemed to fall away into the wind as Lianos sped along and it blew into her face. The surroundings whipped by until they turned into a blur of green and blue; only Lianos's lightly bobbing head was in focus, along with glimpses of his paws as they struck out in front of him. It was like riding on air, a smooth yet turbulent current that could carry her over anything.

Slowly, her tension ebbed away, replaced by exhilaration at the sheer joy of the ride.

He slowed to a trot as they turned onto a trail again. This was more like a horse's trot, except that instead of a two-beat rhythm with diagonal pairs of legs moving in sync, the left pair and right pair hit the ground separately.

"It came this way," he said, pointing with his muzzle at a trail of light-coloured grass where the dew had been disturbed. On the ground there were a few crushed leaves, the indent of a hoof partially visible over one. "But then the scent just dissipates."

Eiryenne left him to ponder where their quarry went while she took advantage of the pause to fit one of the bronze-tipped arrows to her bow. It would be silly, after all, if they got close enough and she wasn't ready.

The dragon paused then swerved into a forest of tall, thin hardwoods. He weaved between their trunks, his head turned down, scanning for both scent and tracks. His claws dented the grass and left deep marks in the dirt. Eiryenne decided that if someone was tracking *them*, their trail would be easy to follow.

The dragon beneath her tensed. He took another sniff. Then he charged.

He'd found the moon kirin's scent.

Here, Lianos was the hunter. His usual light demeanour had changed; there was a new intensity in his eyes as the scent of his prey flooded his nostrils and beckoned to his instincts. The ancient thrill of the chase was pumping through his veins; he leaped through the trees with a deadly purpose, a blur of cerulean and silver.

Up ahead there was a flash of white.

Lianos quickened his step. He hurtled through the tree trunks with such speed that at times Eiryenne almost thought they'd crash into one, but at the last second the dragon would swerve around it, always with just enough space to avoid getting stuck, his wings tucked against his sides snugly to avoid snaring them on anything.

Then the forest became thicker, and at one-point Lianos barged between two ancient redwoods standing quite closely together. He bounced off the side of a trunk, sailing through diagonally to fit. Eiryenne knew he wouldn't make the next gap; the trees here were too dense. He'd get tangled up.

Then the wings on either side of her glowed with blue fire and dissolved into his side, just like the spines. Now unhindered, the blue dragon charged through the trees like a streak of blue lightning. Following his prey, he turned sharply onto a ridge. In the forest the kirin was more agile, but here the advantage was his, since the rocky slope did not slow him down at all. While the kirin's cloven hooves slid and failed to grip the sheet of rock it skidded across at the top, Lianos's claws scraped grooves into the rock to hold him in place and propel him onward.

Over the ridge, the kirin now fled downhill and into the woods again, with the blue dragon hot on its heels.

At first the girl had kept both her arms around the dragon's neck to avoid falling off, but now she straightened on his back and raised her bow.

They dodged an oak to see the moon kirin in full flight over a creek. Eiryenne released her arrow. It flew over the kirin's tail, brushing it. Her next few arrows were even farther off target. She shook her head, trying to concentrate and aim amidst being shaken up and down by the dragon's gait. For a split second the kirin hesitated before it disappeared into a tangle of fallen logs spiked by thick tree trunks. Lianos didn't have time to go around it; he opened his jaws, and a ray of sky-blue flames erupted from his mouth to obliterate the pile.

Leaping over the cinders, Lianos burst into a meadow, his powerful muscles rippling beneath his shoulder scales as his legs pumped ever faster, bringing them closer to their target. His eyes locked onto it.

And there was one moment where the girl was suddenly unsure of where she ended, and the dragon began as she followed his gaze to the kirin and knew his hunger for the kill. Time seemed to slow down. As Lianos took another stride, she aimed. When he reached the peak of his leap, high above the grass, Eiryenne released her arrow. It flew true and hit the moon kirin in the flank. The bronze arrowhead bit deep, and the creature stumbled and hit the ground, rolling end over end. The silvery glow around it faded. Before it had even stopped moving, Lianos was upon it, wrenching its head from its body and reducing the rest to cinders with his fire.

The sudden stop unseated his rider, who was sent flying head over heels just like the kirin. Having had some practice falling off horses, Eiryenne landed rolling by instinct, trying to minimize the amount of damage. She rolled to a stop and sat up, panting. That was the most challenging hunt she'd ever been on, and yet it was also the most exhilarating.

Lianos peered down at her. "Are you okay? Sorry, I should have warned you." The hunter's intensity in his eyes was gone, replaced by the civil, polite persona that Eiryenne was more used to.

"I'm fine," she said, getting up. Her right knee hurt where she'd landed on it, and all of her limbs were sore from clenching the dragon's sides, but otherwise, she was unharmed.

There was a glow of blue fire at his sides, expanding outward as Lianos's wings flickered back into existence.

"I didn't know dragons could do that," she said.

"It's kind of like shape-shifting," he said. "Just on a different scale." He turned and padded into the forest at a more leisurely pace

Eiryenne nodded, thinking back to how she'd seen both dragon and lion mages turn their hands into paws when they were in human form. She followed the dragon through the woods. Though she limped slightly, he didn't offer another ride, and she was not going to ask for it.

"Wait, so Danzi can do that with his spines, too?" And yet she'd spent hours hanging in his claws whenever they flew. Not the most comfortable position, but she'd thought it was the only option.

"If you see Danzi again, do not mention this to him or he will get quite angry," Lianos said.

"I won't," she promised. "He got pretty mad at me when I just asked him whether there were any dragon riders. This book got them confused with wyverns."

"Yes, he *would* be offended by that," the blue dragon said softly. "Don't ask me why. It's not my story to tell."

"You didn't mind, though," she said. "And you knew exactly how many spines to absorb and how to make those ones in front of me soft so I wouldn't impale myself."

He shrugged. "When I was growing up, my best friend was a Dyre wolf."

Eiryenne blinked. "I thought they were evil. I saw so many of them with the Empire."

Lianos looked at her disapprovingly. "That's like saying all humans are evil because Varcroft happens to have a bunch of them working for him."

Eiryenne bit her lip. He had a point.

"Anyway, whenever my friend and I had to go somewhere far or fast, we found it convenient to have him ride me. So, I got used to ferrying him about on my back. It wasn't a big deal to me, you know?"

"So you're used to accommodating a rider. Why hide it from Danzi?"

Lianos sighed. "Danzi and I have very different backgrounds. His opinions were shaped by his own experiences." His tone made it clear that he would not delve into what those were. Maybe he didn't really know, either.

Perhaps he'd answer her original question more accurately instead. "So, *are* there dragon riders, then?" she asked.

Lianos looked thoughtful. "In a general sense, no. The wyverns and horses that humans domesticate are a far cry from what dragons are like. Very few dragons even associate much with other species. Fewer still allow people to ride them. I'm the only one I know of who's accepted riders, and even then, only if needed, never for leisure. Because make no mistake, Eiryenne," he paused to look her in the eye, "dragons are not tame." Again, there was a glint of something wild and even savage in his gaze.

"I have no trouble believing that," she said honestly. Feeling a sudden compulsion, she bowed. "Thank you. That was an honour."

Lianos's scaly lips curved upward, reminding her of the dragon statue in Danzi's crystal cave. "No need for formalities. You know I'm hardly one for them." He chuckled, resonating deep within his chest.

Eiryenne slapped herself on the forehead. Amidst all the excitement of her first dragon ride, she'd forgotten to ask what had happened at the camp.

"So, what happened? Are we under attack?"

"Just a scouting party that got lucky." There was a tree across their path. Lianos grabbed it in his jaws and lifted it out of Eiryenne's way before tossing it aside as easily as he would a twig. "That's the theory, anyway. A bit too lucky if you ask me. But we got almost all of them except for two moon kirin. It's good that we got this one, otherwise it would have carried the camp's location to Varcroft. I just hope the others got the second one."

They soon came to a trail where a mounted patrol greeted them and brought news that the second moon kirin had avoided capture. Here the dragon left her and took to the sky, flying off to check the rest of the forest for the missing kirin while the patrol gave Eiryenne a ride back to camp.

The fence by the meal tent was broken. There was a blackened pile of bodies in black uniforms next to the combat arena. Tents and cabins on the east wing all bore signs of a scuffle. Everyone Eiryenne saw was armed and wary. She was ushered by the patrol elves to where the rest of the kids were gathered around the magic tent.

"Eiryenne!" Leo rushed forward. There was a big scratch on his face, though it was hard to tell whether he'd gotten it during the last attack by Team Blue or by the intruders. "Is it true? I heard you *rode* Lianos!"

"Yeah. We hunted down one of the moon kirin."

"You are *so* lucky," he gasped. "I think I've only seen someone ride him once before, when he and Riard were called on this urgent—"

But Eiryenne thought that what was happening here was more urgent. If the moon kirin were messengers, it would only take one escapee to bring the camp's location to Varcroft. Then they were all in deep trouble.

"Hey," Leo's eyes were distant. He started to stumble. "Can you hear that? That sound?"

"No." Eiryenne looked around. She could hear the wind in the trees and the sounds of concerned campers milling about, but that was it. "What are you talking about?"

"The singing."

A chill ran up Eiryenne's spine.

In a few seconds, however, Leo snapped out of his trance. "What did I miss?" he said eagerly. "I think I zoned out for a second. Hey, the hunter returns." He pointed skyward.

She looked up to see Lianos gliding toward them. Against the sky, it was as if his scales were dozens of tiny mirrors, blending in with the stark azure tone in the background. He passed beneath a few featherlike clouds, the sun's rays only starting to slant now. They lit up both him and the clouds from the side, making both seem to be made of crystal and glowing from within. Cerulean highlights and shadows were passed and caught amidst the glint of his sapphire-like scales, touched with silver where the sunlight struck them at the right angle.

The blue dragon angled his wings and began his descent. The sun just managed to gleam through the thick, translucent blue webbing of his wings, reminding Eiryenne of heavy parchment saturated with blue ink. He flapped them once before landing and folding them up at his sides.

"Any luck?" Yolen asked.

Lianos shook his head. "Wherever it is, it's long gone from here."

Councillor Molekk frowned. "We'll have to send out tracking parties at once. This is outrageous, this is just—*oh, no*." His words caught in his throat as a new shape appeared in the sky.

Around Eiryenne, people were pointing and muttering, looking up as well.

She looked up to see a huge blood-red dragon coasting on the winds with a careless grace, approaching the camp in a slow spiral with great sweeps of his orange wings.

Molekk found his voice again as the red dragon landed next to Lianos. "Archers," he yelled, "take him down."

"Wait, look!" Yolen pointed at something in the dragon's jaws.

It was a moon kirin's head.

"Looking for this?" rumbled the dragon. "What a way to show your gratitude."

"It's Danzi!" breathed Leo.

"Danzi," Eiryenne muttered, "he's back."

"That doesn't matter," screeched Molekk. "I said, *take him down!*"

Danzi looked unfazed. "Greetings," he said to them all. "I just broke into the general's house."

9 ~ Spontaneous Debriefing

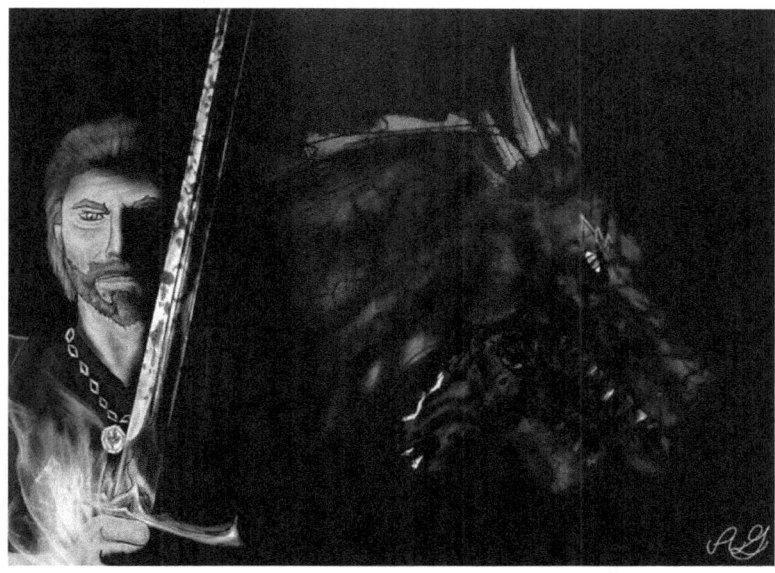

"All right, well I've heard the official version, but I want to know what really happened," Riard said. It was evening, and he, Lianos, Yolen, and Danzi were gathered around the table in Lianos's cabin. After Danzi was questioned and grudgingly released by the Council, they'd decided to hold a debriefing of their own.

"Begin from the start," Lianos said. "They didn't let me in the meeting, after all."

"I went to the capital. Varcroft's entire force was stretched to the maximum between two wars, so it wasn't as difficult to get in as it usually is," Danzi said. "You know, if we had a third army, we could have taken it." He looked thoughtful. "And once we had Irbarvad, the rest of the Empire would slowly crumble."

"You got into Irbarvad," Yolen reminded him. "How on earth—?"

"Like I said, the defences were down. The city was practically empty. A diversion, a minor cloaking spell ..." Danzi trailed off. He wasn't going to tell them about the extent of his plan to invade the capital. It had taken weeks of waiting, strategizing, finding the right chinks in the armour around Varcroft's flagship city. Then, finally, he'd gotten in. Ironically enough, it was Hurraine who'd given him a break as the last of Varcroft's forces were called away to face the Resistance army. And Danzi had crept down the black slope and snuck between the pillars of dark stone, then leaped over the wall and cloaked himself as best as he could.

It wasn't his first visit to the place. He'd been there once as a very young dragon, well before Varcroft's time. It had once been a beautiful place, with striking, sheer mountains and pillars of rock nestling a small, forested valley like a jewel. But now it was covered in decades of grime and filth as Varcroft's minions had carved out their space, destroying the existing Kive town and setting the foundations for what had become the symbol of the Emperor's total power in the region. Vast gates shimmering with layer upon layer of magic stood against walls of black, silver-topped towers.

Danzi hadn't liked it. He didn't like these kinds of cloak-and-dagger missions in general; he was a more directly confrontational kind of being. But with his status of a rogue came the need for deeds such as this. The palace itself was too obvious a target and too hard to reach, nestled in the heart of the city and walled off by sheer cliffs. The general's house was easier.

He'd had a bit of a dilemma in terms of covering his escape, but that matter had been solved before he even reached the house.

"What of Rufus?" Riard asked, referring to the Resistance's main undercover operative in Irbarvad. "You denied coming across him to the Council, but if something's happened to him, then I really need to know, Danzi. You know how many resources we've put into getting a man at the capital."

"Rufus is dead," Danzi said with a shrug. Riard's face fell. "And no, I didn't kill him. I saved his life. Sort of. It's a long story."

"Do tell." Riard rubbed his face, looking grim. In addition to being a valuable operative, Rufus had also been his personal friend.

So Danzi told them how he crossed beneath the shadows of the Timus Bridge that connected the northern half of the city to the south, going underneath and through the chasm to remain undetected. And he'd emerged on the other side to see a pair of mages throttling Rufus. He'd killed the enemy mages only to find that they'd poisoned the Resistance's secret man. Rufus told him he'd been found out. And for the poison, alas, there was no cure.

At this Riard sighed, nodding. His friend had finally met his end at the hands of the Empire.

Lianos gave his brother a look. He knew about the unicorn horn Danzi possessed and how it could cure almost any poison. He also had a sneaking suspicion that if Rufus hadn't been dying when Danzi found him, he'd put him in that condition himself. It was just how he did things. Minor lives like the spy mages were of no consequence if a greater objective could be achieved.

Now that Lianos thought about it, poison seemed a better way to go.

Rufus didn't like Danzi; that had been no secret. But now, faced with death, when Danzi told him his plan, he'd agreed to go along.

"So, I took him to General Khaos's house," Danzi continued. "Just like the rest of the city, it was almost empty." After disintegrating the network of barriers and protective spells surrounding the estate, Danzi had put the twin stone keys to work. One of them he'd gotten from a man named Kafer at a tavern while on the run with the Necklace. The other had been sought by the other members of the Resistance and eventually recovered, brought back to camp upon its discovery. It had been in the parcel he'd snatched before leaving camp last time. Both keys, turned at exactly the right time and with the right incantation, opened the lock. He swung open the heavy oaken doors to reveal a grand corridor and courtyard filled with hidden dangers and traps. "The traps inside were interesting, to say the least." He had a few close calls and had to rely on all of his not insignificant knowledge of magic to get through, mostly unscathed. But brushes with death were part of the dragon's daily routine; they didn't faze him.

Eventually, he reached his prize: the door at the end leading to the general's office. The inner offices were guarded by hellhounds, huge, slobbering demonic dogs with one or more heads filled with an array of gnashing teeth.

"I held the hellhounds at bay and caught them in one of the general's own traps. I brought in Rufus and left him at the table then scattered traces of his magic around the place." Even the table itself was filled with treacherous spells. It took Danzi a couple of minutes to work through them and start opening drawers. He'd found what he was looking for and then some; Varcroft's entire military records for the past seven years. Everyone he did business with, everywhere he had soldiers stationed, his wartime plans, and, most importantly, future strategies. Possibly the greatest single seizure of intelligence the Resistance had ever been presented with. Any hidden base he had, any military suppliers, they'd now know about it all, thanks to Danzi. It was no wonder Molekk was forced to clear him of the death penalty.

"Then what happened?"

"Then," Danzi said with a smirk, "I made things go boom." It was a combination of leeched Khaos magic and the last of Rufus's, with some local explosive mixtures thrown in for good measure. Danzi let it off as soon as he'd backed away and let the hellhounds loose. Despite their ferocity, hellhounds weren't very intelligent creatures. They'd go on a rampage and maul both Rufus and the evidence. Danzi's bomb cleared away any other traces of his magic.

"Hmm. So, it looks like Rufus did it and failed, and the whole place is a mess after the hellhounds, so the documents won't likely to be missed anytime soon?" Lianos said. "Nicely done. Messy, but efficient."

"Exactly; it was messy," Yolen commented. "An expert might still find remnants of your magic after all that. Covering up crime scenes was never your specialty."

"Even if they find out, with Rufus's death and my sporadic record they're more likely to connect it to the Northerners than the Resistance," Danzi continued. "Speaking of which, I also found out that that Tartaway lot want nothing to do with us."

"Been brushing up on finding new allies, Danzi?" Riard looked thoughtful.

Danzi shrugged. "I was in the area. It seemed better to fly up north after the seizure than to risk leaving a trail back to the camp. Besides, I had some other matters to take care of." Namely, hunting Blackthorn. "But anyway, we're at war with the same person. It makes sense to at least explore the possibility."

"But?"

"But Tartawegians are a peculiar lot. All about culture and heritage and the so-called purity of blood. The wrong species, the wrong bloodline even, they can go and sacrifice themselves for all they care. The Northerners are so wrapped up in that nonsense that they'd rather die fighting within their narrow views of honour than associate themselves with those lowly warm-blooded species."

"Remind you of anyone?" Lianos muttered in Draconic. Danzi ignored him.

Riard sighed. "So much for any hope of an allegiance with Tartaway. Unless you know of anything that may change their minds?"

Danzi shook his head. "No. They're very firm in their beliefs. And they made it quite clear," he rubbed his shoulder, where a deep gash made by an icy spear was just starting to heal, "that we are not welcome. Now," he leaned forward, "there is one more piece of information that I withheld from the Council. You will inevitably find out later through other avenues, but …." He frowned. "Yolen? Are you listening?"

The elf had gone rigid. His eyes were blank as his head drooped forward onto his chest. "That voice," he whispered. "What's it saying?"

"Yolen? What's the matter with him?" Lianos stood up.

Danzi frowned. "Our meeting's been breached. Check him."

"Yolen, can you hear me?" Riard asked. He and Lianos both scanned the listless elf with their magic while Danzi checked the perimeter.

"He's clean," Lianos said.

"Perimeter's clear," Danzi confirmed. His frown deepened. "This doesn't make sense."

"The singing. Can't you hear the singing? It's so … so …" Yolen slurred as his words trailed off.

"I don't hear anything," said Danzi. "You're hallucinating. Or experiencing an auditory illusion."

Riard frowned, looking from the dragon mage to the elf. He didn't know which of them had the keener hearing, but both of them could definitely hear better than he could. "It has to be some kind of internal enchantment," he said. "Something very well-contained, something— oh, I hear it." For a second the sound reached his ears as well, and when it did, the table fell away. Or maybe he fell away from the table. Suddenly he wasn't sure which was which.

Then the sound released him, and he found himself lying face-down on the floor, with two dragon mages and a confused elf all looking at him.

Both Danzi and Lianos looked guarded. They were scanning their surroundings with meticulous, all-seeing draconic eyes. But they found nothing.

"What *was* that?" said Lianos as Riard got up.

The mage shook his head. "I don't know. I just went into this trance. I hardly remember a thing. First, I was at my chair, then I was on the ground."

"Hrrrm." Danzi preferred threats that were more direct, something he could sink his teeth into, as opposed to an invisible muscle relaxant. A list of suspects would be hard to compile. Evidently, someone had got wind of their meeting and disapproved of it. And the list of people who disapproved of him being at camp was long. Longer still if he counted outside forces.

Still, their assailants would leave a trail sooner or later.

Riard blinked as the spells he'd put around the cabin to avoid eavesdropping were triggered. But they weren't catching someone who wasn't trying to be seen. "We have visitors. Are you expecting anyone, Lianos?"

"Let's see ... ah, right, that would be Eiryenne and Leo coming for their magic lesson."

Riard let up on the spells, and Lianos did likewise as there was a knock at the door.

"Leo, what are you doing?" They heard Eiryenne's voice. "We should wait until he invites us in—"

Too late. In barged an overexcited blonde elf boy with Eiryenne on his heels, looking sheepish.

Seeing them all, he stopped, looking shocked. Then the grin returned to his face, even wider than before.

"You guys are having a secret meeting? That is so cool."

Eiryenne looked at Lianos. "Er, we'll come back later." She tugged on Leo's arm. "Come on."

But the elf wouldn't budge. "You invaded the capital, broke into the general's house, and waltzed back into camp like it was nothing," he said to Danzi. "That is amazing. How in the world do you do these things? And the look on Molekk's face when he gave you a pardon. And why hasn't the Resistance tried this before, I mean, even if it was supposed to be not doable?"

Eiryenne expected Danzi to brush Leo off, but instead the dragon mage looked amused. "I didn't say it was doable. I just did it."

"We haven't tried it before," Riard said. "Because we seldom have someone of Danzi's knowledge, power—"

"And boredom," Danzi added.

"And motivation," finished the mage. "At our disposal." He glanced at Danzi. "And frankly, I think we still don't."

"What's that supposed to mean?"

"A lot of things." Riard turned back to Eiryenne and Leo. "Now, if you two would just run along now."

"What?" Leo looked crestfallen. "No ..." He trailed off, looking imploringly at his father. It seemed like he'd *never* get to sit in on these top-secret meetings.

Eiryenne had almost succeeded in dragging him out the door when Yolen spoke up.

"Actually," he said. "I think my son is old enough to hear this. If you don't mind, that is." He looked around at the other mages at the table, his gaze lingering on Danzi.

"Can your son keep his mouth shut?" Danzi asked. "Not from what I've seen."

"I can vouch for him," Yolen said. He shot Leo a look. "And you can bet he'll be sorry if he even lets out a peep." The elf boy flinched.

"Very well, Yolen, but on your own head be it," Danzi said firmly.

"Awesome," Leo shouted. Then he put his hands over his mouth. "Sorry," he whispered. Then he glanced at his friend. "What about Eiryenne? Can she stay? I bet she wouldn't say anything to anyone. I mean, she barely even talks about all the stuff she did on her quest."

Danzi met Eiryenne's gaze. Since Leo wasn't bursting with questions about the unicorn horn and crystal cave, he assumed she'd kept those secrets well. After all, not even Riard or Yolen knew about the cave, and they'd be sure to question him about it, Yolen out of curiosity, and Riard out of his sense of duty to ensure that all the

Resistance's assets were well-accounted for and used to what he thought would be their full capacity.

"If you're going to be expanding your circle, now's a good a time as any," Lianos said quietly.

"She can stay," Danzi said after another pause.

Yolen gestured for them to take a seat at the table between him and Riard. He clapped Leo on the shoulder. "Welcome to your first official *unofficial* meeting," he said. "If you know what I mean."

"Right. Secret stuff." Leo was finding it hard to contain himself.

Eiryenne was more cautious. Things were usually secret for a reason, that she knew well. Secrets could be dangerous.

She sat down and looked at the head of the table to where the dragon mages sat. She'd found out a lot about Danzi since he was last at camp. Both as the wandering rogue and, more importantly, the great fallen leader.

He looked almost the same as when she'd seen him last, plus or minus a few new tears in his jacket and some half-healed wounds. The same heavy leather coat with that hidden tint of red, the sharply pointed blonde beard, and those eyes, burning brightly in a face that did little to hide his true nature. All were covered with new bloodstains. Some of it was blue, like the ice mage he'd fought at the Crater.

"Blue blood," she said slowly. "Igarevin?"

He nodded.

"So, either Varcroft found more, or you've been up north."

"Yes," Danzi said slowly. It occurred to him that she'd know about his ulterior motive for going to Tartaway. She'd been there when Blackthorn received the order to go north.

"Tartaway," she said, her thoughts going to the same place. But from what she'd heard, Blackthorn was a touchy subject. Best leave it be. "Yes, I heard they were at war with Varcroft, too. Are they going to help us?"

"No. Fire and ice don't mix, according to them," he said. "Though frankly, I think *both* forces need as much help as they can get when you're up against someone like the Emperor."

"So," Lianos clapped his hands, "before our, er, interruption, you said you had some news for us. Now's a good a time as any."

"Very well." Danzi leaned on his elbows. "Hurraine is dead."

"What?" Leo gasped.

"How?" Riard looked taken aback.

Lianos studied Danzi with his crystal blue eyes, his expression inscrutable. "And her army?"

"Destroyed."

Riard was shaking his head. He looked like he had trouble finding the right words. "Answer me this, then. No, two things. No, three." He looked up, torn between shock and exasperation. "One. Why did you withhold this information from the Council? Two. How do you know this. And three—"

"I flew by the battle site on my way back from Tartaway," Danzi said. He looked solemn. "I saw the Fields of Fetlo stacked with the dead. It was a massacre." The scene had reminded him far too much of Kyrahgrun. Once again, he'd flown over a sea of corpses, and it had been a painful reminder of his own downfall. Maybe if he hadn't lost at Kyrahgrun, Fetlo wouldn't have happened either.

"Any survivors?" Yolen asked softly. He'd known many of those soldiers. They'd been good people.

"Didn't look like it," Danzi said truthfully. "I did see tracks of a small group in the sand heading east, but there was no telling whose they were. Too much blood everywhere. Could've been Imperial soldiers for all we know. Either way, I was being pursued, so I didn' t linger."

"Pursued? By who?" asked Yolen.

"A patrol got lucky."

"And more importantly, where are your pursuers now?" added Lianos.

Danzi licked his chops. "Lunch."

"What I still don't understand," Riard cut in, "is why, *why* you didn't tell the Council this. You do know that by doing that, you're making us all, me especially, do these ridiculous juggling acts between you and the Council's authority?"

"Then stop juggling," Danzi said. "And choose whichever one you think is more important."

There was no reply to that.

"Fine then," he muttered. "Keep up your circus act. But be ready to make a decision when it counts." He looked carefully around at them. "Now, as to why I chose not to inform the Council of this *officially*." He paused. "You know that they pin everything on me these days, from Golenhar's death to chinks in Hurraine's armour to disloyal footmen and unlucky whisky bets." He rolled his eyes. "Now I show up here with word of Hurraine's demise, having been mysteriously absent for the past six months and admit to having been on the battlefield myself after the carnage, with no proof apart from my own word. The Council will have a field day. I don't want that. I have enough *real* blood on my hands, do you understand?"

There was another pause.

"So why *did* you come back?" Eiryenne wasn't sure who the question surprised more, her audience or herself. "If there is nothing for you here, why return?"

Danzi reached inside his jacket and pulled out a tightly bound roll of parchment. He waved his fingers over the seal, which burned with a Draconic symbol before more symbols appeared the length of the silk string binding the parchment, falling away, and retracting until it released the paper.

"You made a copy for yourself," Riard observed.

"Of course. You didn't think I'd hand it all over to Molekk, now did you?" Danzi said, flipping through the pages.

"Where's the scribe that copied it for you?"

"Breakfast."

"What's to say that *those* aren't the originals and what Molekk has a copy?" Lianos said. "I bet there are a few pages in there that you excluded from your official report, too."

Riard frowned. "Now that's a serious offence, Danzi."

The dragon mage smirked slightly. "Unless you haven't noticed, my friend, *everything* I do is rather serious."

Leo peered at the parchment, trying to make out what was written on it, but Yolen tapped his shoulder. "One look in there and your head will be worth a thousand cronos to the Emperor, you got that?" he said.

Leo gulped and looked away.

Lianos studied the pages aloofly as they flashed by his face. He glimpsed a map of the capital, schematics of Varcroft's castle, tactical notes on his army, and planned movements. The cream of the crop. He could already see several annotations in Danzi's handwriting on various plans and schematics. His brother had been busy.

"There." Danzi stopped at a page that showed a map of the Empire. There were different areas circled and labelled as either *checked* or *prospects* and the date that each place had been checked or when it was going to be.

Most of the areas were out east by Turmain and Bremia, some were up around Tartaway, but a few were down south. One of these included, as if by chance, the actual location of the camp.

"It's a map outlining potential Resistance camp locations," Danzi said. "As you can see, our actual location is indeed outlined as a potential candidate, due to be checked next week." This he *had* explained to the Council, but Riard was the only one from this group that had been at the meeting, after all. The rest of them looked surprised to see the map. "I came to warn you. And take the opportunity to potentially put another snag in Varcroft's plans if he does attack here."

"Despite what this map says, we had scouts here *today*," Riard noted.

Danzi shrugged. "It's been several weeks. Varcroft might have changed his plans."

"Someone's coming," Lianos interrupted, looking up. He sensed several Council members approaching the cabin. "Everyone to casual speech in three, two … one."

Riard made a quick sideways gesture with his hand. Both he and Lianos dropped the guard spells around the cabin to avoid arousing suspicion.

Leo opened his mouth to say something, but Yolen covered it. He tapped his ear then pointed at the floor where a wisp of muddy green magic had snaked in underneath the door. Someone was listening in.

In a second, Riard and Yolen were deep in a conversation about the state of the archery range and whether more weapons-oriented practices would benefit the young warriors. Soon they also started discussing how the war games could be improved.

They'd moved their chairs away from the dragon mages. And though their speech sounded upbeat, it was a complete façade. Both were still struggling to deal with the fact that every other Resistance soldier they knew, every friend they had, had been struck down by Varcroft.

"Up for another round of Rajong, brother?" Danzi asked. He was leaning casually back in his chair. "Or will you be content with just three losses in a row?"

"Actually, I think I'll give it another shot," Lianos said. He got up from his chair to grab a box sitting on the side of a shelf.

When Eiryenne had first come to Lianos's cabin, she'd expected something extravagant, maybe because of her impressions of Danzi's cave. But instead, the cabin turned out to be deceptively simple. It had two walls made of stone and two made of canvas, presumably so it could be stretched out and put up to allow Lianos to fit in here in his dragon form. At the centre of the one room was a large, heavy table carved out of blue and white marble, where they were sitting. Unlike Riard's study, the rolls of parchment here were neatly organized and laid out in a steel scroll-holder at the side of the desk, complete with quills and ink. There were candles on the table, little translucent crystals that blazed with light at Lianos's command as he called up a tiny flame in the well at their tops, bathing the cabin in a soft blue glow. He used them whenever the sunlight faded, and he had guests that didn't see as well in the dark as he could.

The back wall was made of interlaced white and blue bricks. In one corner there was a small set of cupboards, smelling strongly of spices. At the solid wall there was a half-empty bookshelf with a few arcane titles laid out alphabetically on the top shelf, while the bottom held knives, polish, and sharpening stones as well as a large, spherical crystal. A sheathed sword hung on a peg on the wall, long and thin, slightly curved, with a heavy tip and a handle wrapped in blue felt. There was a sapphire in the hilt. Below it was another peg on which the dragon mage hung his knives when he wasn't using them.

The only real object of curiosity was the chest tucked in the back left corner next to the blue cot. It was made of a heavy bronze melded with silver, and when Eiryenne put her mage vision to work, she saw how it was locked up with layer upon layer of Lianos's blue fire. Not even anyone from the Council would venture in here. If he had any secret magical trinkets, that was where he must have kept them. But so far Eiryenne had never seen him open it.

Lianos returned to his seat and opened the cardboard box, spilling a bunch of cards onto the table. He and Danzi each took a handful and began to play some kind of card game.

Eiryenne watched as the cards changed, along with the dragon mages' expressions.

"And … got you, ah-ha," Danzi declared triumphantly, smacking his cards down on the table with a grin. Eiryenne realized that unlike the others, he was, in fact, genuinely having fun.

Lianos observed his hand and sighed. "Yeah."

"Is this just a two-player game?" Eiryenne asked.

Danzi waved his hand at the empty seat next to him. "No. The more the merrier."

So, they taught her the rules of the game, and she ended up playing a few hands with them, mostly losing, but it didn't matter. Leo looked on curiously at first, but soon his father had dragged him into his own boring conversation.

In another fifteen minutes or so, even the listeners must have gotten tired of hearing Riard ramble on about the virtues of a camp lifestyle for youngsters' character-building, because the wisp of magic under the door slowly slid back under it and disappeared.

"All clear," Lianos said.

Then the dinner bell rang.

"Ah, good timing," Danzi said, getting up. "Let's go eat."

As they exited the cabin, Riard and Yolen fell away from the others and headed off in different directions. Lianos, too, slid off down a passage between two rows of tents.

"Where are they all going?" Leo asked.

"Dispersing. You don't usually want to linger with the group with which you just had an unofficial meeting," said Danzi. "Just to avoid raising suspicions."

"Oh, right. I get it." Leo looked around suspiciously and then ran off to the side, half-stooped.

"No, he doesn't." Danzi chuckled. "Not yet."

Eiryenne continued to walk beside him. "You seem to be in a good mood," she remarked. It was true that despite the gravity of his news, she'd never seen the dragon mage so light-hearted.

"Of course I am. I just completed the greatest intelligence coup in Resistance history," Danzi said. "Things are moving again." He felt good about his mission. He felt like he was finally *getting* somewhere, that his efforts seemed to have accomplished something meaningful at last. And he liked progress. "One step closer to taking down Varcroft." An eventual end to the endless war.

Hope. That was something Eiryenne hadn't heard in his voice before.

She glanced around then spoke more quietly. "But Hurraine and the army?"

Danzi shrugged. "They weren't getting anywhere under her leadership, anyway. The army's loss I could do without, but that's war for you." He'd tried to distance himself from the army. They weren't his soldiers anymore, after all. And they hadn't been for a long time. Sure, he'd had some allies among them, but he didn't let himself linger on that fact. To Danzi, for years now the battle against the Emperor had consisted of him and him alone. He could go where he wanted, do what he chose. His attachment to any force had to be minimized.

It was his personal successes that were shining in his mind, not the news about the lost army. Having sent Blackthorn into the jaws of several dozen igarevin gave him a certain buzz as well. Vengeance was ever so satisfying. The last he'd seen of that pathetic pegasus was his tail disappearing into the icy maws of the Tartawegian beasts. Never mind that they'd almost gotten him as well. Blackthorn's death was worth it.

It would've been much better if he'd gotten to do it himself, of course. Danzi had lost count of the number of times he'd pictured himself snapping that mangy neck. But a dead Blackthorn was better than an uncatchable Blackthorn.

"What happens to us, though?" Eiryenne's voice broke through his thoughts. "What happens to the camp?"

"That depends on whether Varcroft still deems it worthwhile to seek out our base when he's already destroyed most of the force," Danzi said. "He might just call the Resistance finished and not bother sending men so far south when he's still dealing with Tartaway up north."

"But if he comes?" She sounded nervous. They had no army left to defend them. They were defenceless.

Danzi gave her a look. "Then I'll be waiting."

Eiryenne nodded, realizing she was wrong. They weren't completely defenceless.

They still had the red dragon.

10 ~ The Cry of Chaos

Leo was a little nervous about his new seating arrangement at first. Throughout the summer, he'd gotten used to alternating sitting either between Roben and Nur or Eiryenne and Grindt. Today, his elf friends had promised him dibs on an exclusive archery club meeting run by the sentries; it was all they could talk about for the past few days. They were expecting him to come over and start raving about it. But now Roben and Nur's invite seemed bland compared with all the exciting secret stuff he'd just learned. What sucked most was that he couldn't say a word to them about it. If he did, his dad would kill him. And Danzi would be mad. He wasn't sure which was scarier.

So, he'd waved his other friends aside, drawing puzzled looks, and followed Eiryenne instead. She'd sat next to Danzi without hesitation, and they were now chatting away about something or the other. Leo wished he could be that casual around the formidable dragon mage. Walking up to them and asking if he could sit down had to be the scariest thing he'd done all summer, Nur's dare aside.

But Danzi seemed less uptight than usual and hadn't minded. Still, Leo sat down next to Eiryenne and took a steadying breath.

She patted him on the arm. "You okay?"

"Yeah, just …" He made a gesture in front of his face, trying to find the right words. "So. Much. Stuff." He felt like he was going to burst. Danzi breaking into the capital. The secret plans. The resistance inside the Resistance. Hurraine, dead. The army, dead. It was almost too much to take in.

"So how are you finding camp?" Danzi asked, taking a sip of his cider.

"It was a bit of a rough fit at first," she admitted. "But I found my way. And I guess it's become kind of like home now." She paused. "And your suggestions worked, by the way. About what to do with certain people." She hadn't even looked at Kevrina's table since they came in. She didn't matter anymore. Especially not in light of these recent, more serious events.

"Of course they worked." Danzi smirked. "The theory is sound. It's a matter of applying it right." He nodded his approval.

Leo wasn't listening. "But that means, " he muttered, "Nur's dad. Tukse's brother. Ehen and Bursair. They're all dead and I can't even tell them. And my cousin—"

"That's the price of secrecy," Danzi told him. "You were warned."

"Yeah, but, " Leo fell silent as a chubby figure waddled up to them. It was Grindt. Leo frowned. That boy was never late for dinner.

He wasn't dressed for it, either. There was a pack on his back and a padded jacket across his shoulders; his short sword was strapped to his belt.

"Are you going somewhere?" Eiryenne asked.

His face was grim. "I've been drafted off," he told them, looking at the ground.

Leo's jaw dropped. "What? Where?"

"They're sending a team into the Empire," Grindt mumbled. "And I'm on it. We're heading off in ten minutes."

The elf was aghast. "But why would they pick *you*?"

"I don't know! I didn't exactly volunteer for it. You both know how I feel about these kinds of things." Grindt's lip was trembling.

"But what the heck —"

"More importantly," Danzi cut across him. "Who assigned you to this mission, and what does it entail?"

Grindt blinked as if just noticing him for the first time. "Oh, Councillor Molekk did, about fifteen minutes ago. They had a meeting about it and called us in. I dunno what we're supposed to do or where we're going; they said we'd get further orders once we were inside."

Leo opened his mouth, but Danzi raised a hand. The elf closed it again.

Grindt raised an eyebrow. This was new; people usually couldn't shut up Leo so easily.

"I see." Danzi looked thoughtful. So, the Council had met without Riard and acted outside of his knowledge. Not a very promising sign.

The chubby boy turned his attention back to the two kids. "So yeah, I just ... came to say goodbye, I guess."

"Have fun," Leo said. "You know I'm jealous."

"Good luck," Eiryenne said earnestly. "Don't worry about it. You'll be fine. See you when you get back."

Someone called out Grindt's name. He turned away and followed a group of elves and Kive, all lead by a large minotaur, and they headed toward the gate.

Danzi got up from his seat. "Interesting. I'm going to go see what Riard knows about this." He turned and disappeared between rows of tents and cabins.

"I guess they found out about the meeting," Eiryenne said. "Or maybe they didn't. Riard's always been on Danzi's side, more or less, whenever he came here. I think they're just starting to not trust him anymore, or ...." Something was wrong, but she couldn't put her finger on it. A chill on the breeze, a silence in the air.

Silence. Why had there been silence for several minutes when Leo normally had trouble keeping his mouth shut for more than half a second?

Eiryenne turned to see the cup fall from Leo's hands and land on the table with a clatter, spilling. For a second he went limp, his head lolling to one side. Then it snapped upright as he went rigid.

"Leo?"

The elf's eyes were vacant, unfocused. Then he turned his blank gaze on her and blinked twice. He raised his hand.

"Horali sogal!" he shouted. A yellow light burst from his outstretched arm and flew at Eiryenne, knocking her over.

"Leo, what are you doing?" she yelled, scrambling to her feet, and clutching the shoulder she'd fallen on.

He ignored her and continued to speak incantations. She caught his subsequent spell on a barrier then focused her energy and hit him in the chest before he could finish his next one. Not waiting for him to recover, she ran.

As she rounded a pair of tables, she almost ran right into Roben.

"Roben," she said breathlessly. "Leo's gone mad. I think you better—"

But she broke off as he muttered under his breath and sent a glowing rock hurtling at her chest. She caught it with her magic at the last moment, deflecting it back at him and continuing to run.

Screams reached her ears, and Eiryenne looked up to take in the rest of the scene. Her jaw dropped. The entire clearing was filled with chaos. Cassandra was screaming as Larkden and Nur chased her around the table, shooting spells at her. Her hair was on fire. Kevrina and Tukse were duelling by the meal tent while a minotaur fought Hilla in front of the councillors' table.

What on earth was going on?

She ducked beneath a minotaur's swinging arm before tripping over someone's unconscious body. Eiryenne fell hard, but the trip saved her a lot of damage; a dagger glistening with Leo's yellow magic embedded itself into the table where her head had been a second before. He was in pursuit and gaining.

Eiryenne scrambled to her feet and sent a mental enchantment toward the grass at Leo's feet. It twisted up and around his calves, tangling him. She was about to send another spell when she sensed a purple blast of magic whistling toward her. It effortlessly shattered her barrier, along with the table she crouched behind.

The girl peered out from the shambles of the table. It was Leo's uncle, Fraskis. He was about to cast another spell, but then Nultela, Leo's aunt, stepped into view, and he turned on her instead.

Eiryenne blinked. Whatever this was, it had gotten the adults, too. Her horror only doubled when she looked at the councillors' table to see Molekk and the others standing on their chairs, magic streaming from their hands as they attacked the kids.

She got up and continued to run, ducking beneath spells and casting counter-spells without looking back. She got to the edge of the clearing and sprinted between the tents, many of which were burning.

She rounded the corner and bumped into Tina. The shepherd had her short sword out.

"Oh, no," Eiryenne muttered, gathering magic in her palms. "Not you, too."

"You're not under the spell?" Tina asked, lowering her sword.

"And you're not?"

"No," Tina said. "I still have my mind. Those others, they're like drones. Won't answer questions or talk. They just attack."

"Oh, the whole camp's gone insane," Eiryenne burst out. "What do we do?"

"At the moment … run." Tina pointed over Eiryenne's shoulder to where Leo was approaching them, light flashing from his palms. Riard and Nur were hot on his heels.

Eiryenne shuddered. She'd have a hard enough time handling Leo or Nur; she'd never be able to hold an experienced mage at bay on her own.

With her mage vision, she saw Riard gathering a complex net of green light and start to shape it into some kind of advanced spell. Whatever it was, Eiryenne didn't want to be on the receiving end of it.

They needed a distraction. Now.

Eiryenne concentrated, pulling as much of the other mages' magic away from them as she could. Riard's focus was too tight, but Leo and Nur yielded quite a bit of elvish magic before they realized what was happening and clamped down on the connection. Then Eiryenne thought of fire and blinding light and set all her energy into one word not taught by instructors in class but embedded into her memory by experience.

"*Raikuro!*"

Light exploded to their right, illuminating the night with a dazzling display of yellow, blue, purple, and white. It flowed from Eiryenne to blind the other mages. She just managed to duck behind a cabin with Tina. Safe in the shadows, they continued to run.

"In here," Eiryenne said as they reached her cabin. Well, technically it wasn't hers, but she'd been using it ever since her original bunk had been pranked; she still didn't care to sleep under the same roof as her tormentors.

Shutting the door behind them, Eiryenne let out a breath.

"That was an impressive light show," Tina said.

"I learned from the best." Eiryenne rummaged in her packs for her sword, bow, and dagger, putting them all on and checking her quiver. "But it won't disorient them for long. We'll have to keep moving. I can't hold them all off by myself."

"I think we should drop by the meal tent again," Tina said.

"What? I was about to suggest that we find the quickest route out of here." Though if she were honest with herself, Eiryenne knew it wasn't likely they'd be able to slip under the noses of so many powerful mages.

"We can't be the only ones unaffected by whatever this enchantment is," Tina said. "You said it yourself; they're too much for you alone."

Eiryenne nervously fingered the hilt of her sword. She really hoped that she didn't have to use it. Or her bow. She'd thought it would be terrible to lose a friend in battle and now she found the prospect of killing them herself even more dreadful.

He brings death everywhere he goes.

Eiryenne blinked. Where had she heard those words?

Chaos shadows the red dragon's footsteps.

The man at the tavern in Loturg, back where she first met Lianos. That man had spoken while watching Danzi beat up someone named Kafer to get a weird stone key.

Why were those words coming back to her now?

Maybe, said a voice in the back of her head, *maybe it was because everything was fine before Danzi came back.*

Eiryenne shook her head. "What if it's contagious?" she said. "I don't know about you, but I don't fancy having my mind stolen from me."

Tina shrugged. "We have to try."

She was right. The crazed mages were searching the camp, and they were getting closer. Eiryenne could sense their magic shining brighter in her awareness. She'd used up most of her magic already, and she wouldn't stand much of a chance if they were caught again.

She took a deep, steadying breath. "All right. Let's go."

They crept out of the cabin. Sticking to the shadows, they crept along the row of tents.

The first to find them, fortunately, was not a mage. It was a boy from Eiryenne's combat practice. She'd sparred him once but didn't know his name. He came at them with a roar. Eiryenne, tired from her magical exertion, stayed back while Tina crossed swords with him. They parried back and forth a few times before the shepherd hit him in the head with the hilt of her sword, knocking him out.

Their next bespelled assailant, however, was Stroman.

Tina readied her sword, but Eiryenne put a hand on her shoulder.

"Don't bother," she said quietly. It seemed that her magic was once again required.

The only problem was she barely had any left, and the combat instructor was moving toward them at an elf's speed, enormous broadsword held aloft.

Eiryenne grabbed the last scraps of magic in her reservoir and strung them together, grabbing more from her sword, before sweeping it out with her mind and forming a tangle that snared Stroman's legs, binding them together, and then collapsing a tent on him. She thanked her lucky stars that he didn't have magic, or she'd never stand a chance.

The main fight had moved from the meal tent up toward the combat arena, with pairs of fleeing kids also scattered throughout the rest of the camp.

"Know any invisibility spells?" Tina asked as they crouched in the shadows of a burned-down cabin.

"No. And even if I did, they wouldn't be strong enough to hide us from this lot," Eiryenne muttered.

"Can you tell which ones are mad?"

Eiryenne shifted her gaze to mage vision and scanned some of the rampaging teens. "No. They all look fine."

"All right, then," Tina muttered, taking stock of the situation. "So far, no one under the spell has talked back. They also move a bit rigidly. Look for people acting naturally."

Eiryenne observed the scene. Larkden was still chasing Cassandra around some tables.

"Oh my god, what is wrong with you?" she screamed. Her hair was charred. "Leave me alone, you little freak."

Eiryenne rolled her eyes. Great. So far, the only one apart from her and Tina that seemed to be sane was a magic-less diva.

"Cassandra's definitely still herself," she said. "Not that that helps us much."

She looked over at Tukse and Kevrina, still blasting magic at one another and demolishing the tents surrounding them. They were closer to the combat arena now and fought closely beside Leo's aunt and uncle. At times Kevrina and Leo's aunt appeared to be working together, fighting back-to-back and occasionally spitting insults at their opponents.

"Those two, I think," she muttered, pointing.

"All right, so we have Leo, Riard, Nur, Larkden, Tukse, Stroman and Molekk on the list of hostiles," Tina said. "Cassandra, Kevrina, Aunt Nultela, you and me are so far sane." She paused. "I don't like our odds."

They fell silent as a minotaur passed them.

Eiryenne frowned. There had to be a pattern here. What did all the victims have in common? Maybe it was some place they'd all visited during the war games, or, more likely, some enchanted food they'd all eaten during dinner, or maybe it really was just random. The luck of the draw at play as some convoluted enchantment wreaked havoc on the minds of those at camp, striking at the first people it came across.

Surely, they'd detect something so powerful coming. Eiryenne knew there were all kinds of protective enchantments and barriers on the camp.

A memory from earlier that day came back to her. "Listen," she said. "Larkden, Leo, and Grindt all acted strangely at some point during the war games. They kept on saying they heard some kind of song when there wasn't one."

"A song? That's odd."

Eiryenne watched as Aunt Nultela put up a barrier and began herding kids into the combat arena.

A song only some people could hear. A song that enchanted and made people lose their minds. Suddenly Eiryenne remembered a page from Hayden's storybook that dealt with creatures who did exactly that. Though the storybook hadn't exactly been accurate so far, it usually supplied the general gist of the monster.

Eiryenne gulped. "Tina," she said. "I think I see the pattern. They're all male. Tell me, are there such things as sirens?"

The shepherd frowned. "I've only heard rumours of them. Supposedly, the sound of their song is enough to drive any man insane. Wait, are you saying?"

She was cut off as the minotaur came around again, spotting them this time and launching a log at their heads. Eiryenne ducked beneath it and grabbed Tina's arm.

"Get to the arena," she said, starting to run. She paused to knock Larkden aside and shoving Cassandra in the direction of the arena. Eiryenne continued to run, passing by a pair of fighting shapeshifters who'd taken on their true forms, cats like lions, but smaller and covered with spots. Leopards.

One of them turned and bounded after her. But then it passed her, and Eiryenne realized that it, too, was running for the arena.

They both just managed to get through the doors before Nultela slammed them shut and muttered something in Elvish. A film of magic, glowing with the colours of many different mages, rose to envelop the arena.

It was evident that Leo's aunt had come to the same conclusion as Eiryenne, because as she looked around, it seemed like the camp's entire female population was crammed onto the dusty field. Some of the girls stood in huddles, hugging one another, a few were panicking and rolling around in the dirt in tears. Others were doubled over in shock, still panting from their run. Almost all bore minor injuries of some kind.

Looking around, Eiryenne realized she didn't blame them one bit. She was just as scared as they were. But as more and more blasts of magic bombarded the arena's barrier, she also knew that something had to be done, or they'd all perish in here.

There was a loud crack as a wave of green magic crashed into the barrier. Cassandra and Taymel both yelped and jumped up, clutching each other, and shaking.

Eiryenne kneaded her forehead. Great, just great. They were pitted against some of the strongest fighters in the Resistance, and all they had were a bunch of scared, witless teenage girls.

"All right, girls, pull yourselves together," shouted Nultela. The place quieted only a little, screams replaced by loud sniffling.

"Can someone *please* tell me what's going on?" demanded Hilla. Her hair was burned off on one side of her head, and her arms were covered in scrapes. She looked shaken but outraged.

"We appear to have a siren problem," said Nultela.

"Sirens?" burst out Cassandra. "What's that supposed to mean? What's wrong with everyone?"

"That means that every man in this camp is being controlled," said the elf woman. "Doesn't matter the species; if it's male, his mind belongs to the sirens. They must've been setting this up for a while now. There have been reports of men spontaneously fainting this past day or so. You girls won't be able to hear the siren's song. We're immune."

"You mean it's just us?" Taymel voiced the sentiment going through all their heads. "But what are we supposed to do?"

Nultela shrugged. "I don't know, but we better figure it out soon. I activated the combat arena's emergency protection barrier, but it won't last long." A handful of buildings and structures in the camp had this feature, set in by all the mages beforehand in case of an attack. They'd never imagined it being put to this kind of use, though.

"Kill the sirens." A new, guttural voice spoke up. Eiryenne was mildly surprised to see a minotaur in the room; even more so to see the purple Council badge on its grey toga. That had to be Councillor Ha, the minotaur ambassador. Eiryenne had seen Ha before, but she didn't realize it was a lady minotaur. Now that she thought about it, maybe Ha did look a bit less hairy than the other minotaurs Eiryenne had seen around camp.

"We reach the sirens and kill them. Give the others back their minds," Ha continued.

"Can't do a direct attack, though," Nultela said, looking around the room. "And how will we find them? They could be anywhere. We can't hear their song, so we can't tell where it's coming from."

Eiryenne studied the people in the arena, doing a mental head count. Aside from Nultela, only a couple of other elves and Kive women rounded out their adult mage count. There were also some magic-less humans, Tina, of course, then old Laurel, who spun tapestries, and two women who were cooks.

As for the kids, there was the familiar gaggle of Taymel, Cassandra, Hilla, Mels, and Kevrina, as well as a few elf girls Eiryenne wasn't familiar with, and a handful of shapeshifters like the leopard who stood at the edge of the pack, grooming herself.

Eiryenne clapped her hands. "Come on, girls," she said, trying to sound encouraging. "We can do this. We'll need a distraction to get past the guys around the arena, but then we can split up into teams and search the camp for the sirens."

Nultela frowned at her with some distaste, but she nodded. "Let's go, then! Organize yourselves into squads of four. At least one mage per group." She then looked around at the other adults. "We'll make a distraction so that you can slip through." She paused as protests and cries rang out throughout the arena. "No complaining. I don't want to hear your whining. This is what you were trained for. Or were supposed to be, anyway. Now hurry up." Then she turned to Ha and lowered her voice. "This barrier won't be able to hold back the dragons. Be ready."

The girls muttered among themselves and began to shuffle around, looking for all the world as if they were moodily choosing partners for a boring combat exercise.

As Kevrina quickly scooped up her friends into a group, shouting, "Team Pink!" Eiryenne looked around. Soon the other girls had picked up her lead and were calling out team colours. It might have been a good idea until they started bickering over what colours were best.

"Never mind that," Nultela scolded them. "Now, you four, you'll be a team and search the northeast quadrant of camp."

Eiryenne checked her sword belt before straightening. "Team Red," she called out. "Who's in?"

Tina came over and clapped her on the shoulder. "Let's do this."

"I'll go." Eiryenne looked over to see the leopard that had raced her to the gate. Her fur, coloured cream where it wasn't overlaid by black markings, was matted and dirt-splattered, and her ears were bleeding quite badly. But there was a determined expression on her furry muzzle. "I want to save my brother."

"We'll save him," Eiryenne reassured her, though she sounded far more confident than she felt. And since her magic was starting to return, she used what she had to heal the leopard's ears and fix one of the more severe cuts on another girl.

No one else was going toward them, so Eiryenne decided they'd make do with just three. They'd move quicker that way anyhow.

There were more hits on the barrier. It crackled and bent but held, though it was becoming clear it wouldn't hold much longer.

Nultela and the other women were now having a brief discussion about what they were going to do. They weren't feeling very hopeful; the men outnumbered them by far. It was going to be a tough battle.

Then the blasts of magic quieted, and there was a new sound at the gate.

It took a few seconds for Eiryenne to realize that it was knocking. Someone was knocking on their door.

"Hello?" called a voice, muffled by the wood and the magic. "Can we come in?"

"What are you doing?" came a second voice. "People *never* answer their doors during a siege. You should know better."

"It's worth a try."

"Who is this?" called out Nultela. "Unless you are a woman coming to join us or a siren coming to surrender, you aren't getting through those doors."

Silence.

"Very well."

Then there were more blasts of magic against the barrier, followed by bright flashes of light.

Nultela frowned. "They're starting to break through. All right, girls—" But she was interrupted by an explosion up above. The fabric of the barrier was broken open by twin jets of orange and cerulean flames. And through it flew the dragons, shimmering like moving statues of ruby and sapphire.

Eiryenne gasped, stumbling back. They were too late. Nothing could stop those two.

Danzi and Lianos swooped down toward them on wings brimming with fire. Their own blazing barriers easily deflected the frantic spells that Nultela and the others were now casting at them.

"Dragons," Cassandra screamed. "How do we fight *dragons*?"

"Short answer? You don't," rumbled Danzi.

"We come in peace," shouted his brother. Though coming from a roaring mouth filled with enormous triangular teeth, it didn't sound very convincing. And they must have realized that, because, still keeping up a protective barrier of flames, both dragons shifted into their human forms.

"We come in peace," repeated Lianos, his voice quieter in this form and not quite as deep, as if lacking that cavernous, guttural echo.

"You're lying," shouted Nultela, her face contorted in a disgusted frown.

"Well, they're not exactly fighting back, now are they?" Tina said.

She had a point; the dragons had only repelled the mages' spells, not retaliated. Otherwise, they'd all be swimming in a sea of fire right about now.

"It is trickery of the sirens," Nultela said, shaking her head and still not lowering her glowing sword.

"Siren songs don't work on us," Danzi said.

"And we did try knocking," Lianos pointed out.

"So, you're … un-sirenable?" Eiryenne asked.

"Something like that."

"No, it is not possible," the elf woman retorted. "There are *no* un-sirenable species."

Danzi winked at Eiryenne. "I think you just coined a new word."

"The song works on *all* males of *all* species," Nultela continued. You're not female, now are you?"

"No," Lianos agreed. "But you see, the thing is, technically, we're not really male either."

"What?" Now Nultela looked *really* confused, an expression mirrored by most of the others.

"But you've got beards and everything," Cassandra said. "And deep voices."

Danzi shrugged. "All dragons have deep voices."

Lianos tugged at his beard. "Our faces alone may *appear* male in human form, but you've got remember that as with any shape-shifter, this is just a reflection of the species we're imitating. It's superficial; an avatar. Technically, dragons have no true gender."

Now the women and girls were staring at them with weird looks, as if the thought were too much to process.

"O … kay." Nultela looked puzzled. "But—"

"Now that we've cleared that up," Danzi interrupted. He didn't know why the foolish *pyerems* always found that so hard to comprehend. He raised his hands, and fire pooled out to fill the hole that he and Lianos had created in the barrier. "There's the matter of sirens to deal with."

"We were planning to split up and search the camp in a grid pattern," explained Eiryenne. "To find the sirens and neutralize them."

"Can you hear their song, at least?" Nultela inquired.

Danzi shook his head. "No."

"Then we'll stick to the plan," the elf woman said. "At least we'll have some more cover with you two. They've always sung praises of your power, dragons. Let's find out just how good you are."

Lianos frowned. Killing was one thing. Keeping them at bay without hurting them, well ….

Nultela looked around. "Ready? On three. One …"

The barrier surrounding the arena collapsed, and men began to jump the walls.

"Three," Danzi shouted, blasting fire.

The women scattered under the cover of the dragons' fire, the squads running off to search their areas.

Lianos crafted a barrier of blue fire, hitting the men as carefully as he could, trying to repel them with the heat rather than burn them with his magic. Danzi was engaged with Riard and Leo's uncle Fraskis, blocking their rays of green and yellow magic with his own fiery orange aura.

Nultela and the other women were engaged in the fight as well. But the other mages were forcing them back into the corner of the arena. Several of the girls' squads, including Teams Red and Pink, had been cornered as well.

"We have to move them out of here," Lianos said. "Take it outside." He shape-shifted and sent a wave of blue fire splashing around the girls, forcing the other mages back.

Danzi took something out of his pocket as he tackled Tukse to the ground. It was a fist-sized crystal, flecked with blue. He shoved it against the elf's head, then tapped it and frowned. "Not clear enough," he growled to himself. "Unless." He looked thoughtful. "We need to find the first point of contact, the anchor."

"Take this," he said to Eiryenne, tossing her the crystal. "You know what it does. There will be one man with a cloudy aura over his magic. Find him and put it in his hand."

Frasksis was launching greenish yellow bolts of magic at the group, which bounced off Danzi's fire. Instead, it hit the earth around them, shrivelling it and turning the plants to dust. Whatever spell that was, Eiryenne was glad that she didn't find herself on the receiving end. But he and the other mages continued to attack, driving spell after spell toward them and any who tried to leave the arena.

Danzi shifted to his true form. Glowing fire flowed out of both dragons' open mouths, aiming at the male mages, hitting the earth at their feet, and forcing them to retreat. Their magic pooled and spread until it formed a sort of fiery cathedral, half icy blue, half blazing orange, flickering with white where the magic touched. It stretched from the doors of the arena out into the night.

Recognizing their cue, Eiryenne grabbed Tina's arm. "Now!"

Together with the leopard, they sprinted down the fiery pathway, flashes of the other mages' magic hitting the dragonfire in thunderous clashes of light as they went. But the spell held, and they were unscathed. The rest of the girls and women followed their lead. The dragons themselves emerged from the arena soon after, flying overhead and taking the fight with the mages back to the meal tent. Behind them, the combat arena exploded.

They were drawing out all the men, Eiryenne realized, so that there would be none left to defend the sirens.

She cringed as they passed one singed body after another. These people weren't supposed to be injured or dead. They were supposed to be on their side.

Gritting her teeth, she and her posse plunged on through wrecked tents and burning cabins to the west row they'd been assigned.

They didn't get far before a shining arrow whizzed by Eiryenne's head to hit the leopard in the flank.

She blinked in surprise. They'd never even heard it coming. Turning, Eiryenne saw Leo crouching in the grass, his longbow out and gleaming with his fluorescent yellow magic. Behind him was Larkden, his endless but ineffective incantations continuing to flow from his lips.

Leo fired again, and Eiryenne raised her hand, meaning to blast the arrow out of the air like she'd seen Danzi do. Instead, it only altered its course by a few inches, grazing her other cheek.

While she engaged Leo, Tina pulled the arrow from the yowling leopard's flank. Then they both rushed Larkden.

Eiryenne looked up briefly before returning to her duel and putting up a fresh barrier. But something made her look back.

Larkden's magic was grey. It was always grey. But it was usually pearly grey. Now there was a tint to it, ever so slight and easy to miss. It was a shade darker now, a stormy steel grey.

The anchor.

11 ~ The Siren's Scream

"Are you seeing this?" Lianos asked, pointing with his muzzle.

Danzi nodded. There was something different about Yolen compared with all the other possessed men. Something sentient in his gaze, some kind of shadowy tint over his magical energy. "Grab him."

Yolen sent a jet of yellow light billowing out toward Danzi, who matched it with his fire then increased the flow until it knocked the elf right over. Instantly, both dragons leaped at him, shape-shifting and pinning him to the ground. Lianos had his left arm and was holding it down with glowing fingers, sealing off his magic. Danzi was doing the same to the right side. They had to be careful not to hurt him. It might have only taken one dragon mage to kill him, but it took two to hold him down safely.

The elf continued to struggle, but Danzi had him pinned with a knee across the chest to restrict his movement. Then he shoved another chunk of crystal into the elf's hand. It was the same, blue-flecked kind as the ones in his cave, the naturally occurring magic within that allowed whatever someone pictured in their head to be reflected in the crystal. It hadn't worked with the other men; their minds were too far gone. But now, an image appeared on the polished surface: two glowing figures standing on a dais. They were shaped like women in flowing dresses, each with a pair of angelic wings. One had black hair, the other blonde. Their mouths were open in song.

Danzi frowned. He recognized the black-haired siren. "Where is that?"

His brother studied the image. It was focused on the sirens—hardly any part of the surroundings was visible. Not much to go on. "Can't you make it zoom out or less magnified?"

"No."

Lianos racked his brains. Then it came to him. "That's right. The temple!"

Both dragons shape-shifted and took to the sky, leaving behind a trail of men with their hair on fire and minotaurs chasing their own burning tails. Lianos led them toward the heart of the camp. Danzi hadn't seen any temple there.

"Temple? There's a temple at the camp?"

"It was here when we first built the camp," Lianos said. "They levelled the area and built over top of it, but if I'm right—"

"They converted the structure into a hidden, underground fort like Kaydale?"

"Yup."

At the heart of the camp, beside the two-storey fort that served as the main base, there was a sloping hill that disguised the hidden temple. There was already a crack in the hillside. Team Red had been here. And judging from the scents, so had Team Pink. Evidently there'd been two anchors.

Meanwhile, inside the hill that had turned out to have a secret passageway leading to a whole network of tunnels, Eiryenne's team was following Kevrina's as they made their way through the stony maze. Eiryenne had seen the dais in the crystal when she pressed it to Larkden's forehead, but no one on her team had known where that was. So, she'd asked the nearest other team. Unfortunately, that had been Team Pink. Fortunately, Hilla had recognized the design. Her mother had worked in the temple before it was destroyed. Some old Kive stuff. Boring things, she'd insisted.

The passageway was dark and damp. Water sloshed at their feet.

"It's *cold*," whined Cassandra.

"Shut up," growled Hilla. She lit the way with a floating sphere of her purplish magic.

Eiryenne was saving her own magic for the confrontation. She ended up tripping over something in the dark puddles and almost falling on her face.

"Klutz," muttered Kevrina. "Should've left you all behind. We can handle this ourselves."

"Yeah, like you could clearly handle all the guys in the arena yourselves," said Eiryenne.

"Now is no time for this," Tina cut in. "We need to stick together." The words were barely out of her mouth before she plunged through the water with a scream and disappeared.

"Tina?" Eiryenne gasped.

An icy chuckle filled the air. "Oh, she was always so afraid of drowning," a woman's clear voice rang out, echoing off the musty stone walls.

"What about this one?" came a second voice. "Little Cassandra. Oh, so vain. Such foolish pride. Such fear."

Suddenly, Cassandra screamed. She dissolved into shadows.

But Eiryenne found that she could still sense Cassandra's life force nearby, though she couldn't see it. It was hidden from her behind some kind of magical veil. Concentrating to turn on her mage vision, she saw a tendril of wispy, almost colourless magic reach out for Taymel, though Cassandra remained hidden.

"Taymel. Oh, what a mess," the voice continued. "You'll do anything to fit in, won't you?"

She was the next to disappear, this time in a flurry of pink magic. The leopard followed shortly after.

"It's some kind of spell," Eiryenne whispered to the others. "Watch out." She pushed out a wave of her own magic, which collided with the spindly tendrils of what had to be siren magic. But they began to wade through it with barely a pause.

Then Kevrina and Hilla added their own power to the mix, and the barrier appeared to hold. Standing back-to-back, the three girls panted with the energy it was taking out of them to hold up the spell.

"Ah, why? Why so futile, girls?" the voice came. "Why not just give in to the inevitable? You know you're all going to die here."

"Because," panted Eiryenne, "resistance matters."

"I am *so* kicking your butt once this is over with," muttered Hilla. "We should've never followed you in."

"Hey, just so you know, I'm not any happier with this situation than you guys are," the girl replied. "You know what we should've done? Called the dragons." It was stupid, of course, to have thought that they could handle this by themselves. But when they'd looked in the crystal, two unarmed sirens hardly seemed like a problem.

"Hilla," the sirens called, their voices flowing together in a single chilling note.

The Kive girl suppressed a shudder.

"Proud and determined. But so flawed. So afraid. The girl born with the Sight who sees nothing. Aren't your parents disappointed?"

"Shut up," the Kive girl whispered. "Just shut up!" She chucked a glowing knife toward the sound of the voices.

"Belittling others to cover up your own failings. Shame, Hilla, shame," continued the sirens. "For it is true, just as your mother foretold, you will die by your own hand." The knife flew out of the darkness to embed itself in Hilla's chest. She gasped, just once, then collapsed.

"Is she dead?" gasped Eiryenne.

"I don't know. Don't break the circle!"

Now it was just Eiryenne and Kevrina left, struggling to keep the sirens out.

"I'm trying."

"We can feel your fear." Now the shadows lifted somewhat, and two figures appeared, side by side, floating in the mist. They looked like women with skin that glowed and wings with white feathers, wrapped in silky dresses that appeared to be no single colour for more than a second. Both laughed at the girls' terror.

"Kevrina. The last of the doomed bloodline," said one of the sirens, the one with jet-black hair. Her blonde sister continued to chuckle.

The girl frowned. "What?"

"Misguided. Arrogant. And always chasing that elusive vanity. It's never good enough for you, is it?" the siren paused. "Nothing is. Nothing will be. Your reflection will never be what you truly desire it to be. And your apathy ... you don't care much for the Resistance, now, do you?"

Eiryenne frowned. She sensed that this talk was going in a different direction. And something told her she wouldn't like where it was headed.

"We can give you what you crave," said the siren. "Beauty. Power. What would you give up for that, Kevrina Throtingale?"

Kevrina opened her mouth to say something, starting to lower her magical defences. But Eiryenne poked her in the ribs, hard.

"Don't listen to them," she said.

"Ah, *Eiryenne.*" She couldn't help but feel a chill run up her spine as the creatures turned their attention to her. Two sets of ageless, liquid brown eyes fixed themselves on her face. Somehow, they made her look up and meet their gazes.

"You think yourself so brave and valiant," said one of the sirens. "But inside you are still filled with fear. That voice of doubt at the back of your head, threatening darkness, telling you you're still that little, ugly orphan that no one wants. That voice is right."

"Stop it."

"So much hope, but so misplaced and fragile," added the second siren. "Just waiting to be broken. And beneath that there is only fear and panic and the raw anxiety that will tear your mind apart. You are nothing. You don't even have a last name. You're just a word. A tiny, troubled mind, teetering on the brink of panic."

Eiryenne sucked in a deep breath. Somehow, their words needled her in a way that they never should have been able to. She shook her head, trying to tell herself that they were wrong.

But she couldn't. Because they were all too true.

"We know your every thought," crooned the sirens. "We know your deepest fears and darkest desires."

"And of fear, there is so much," one continued. "You fear darkness, and death, and fire and loss, and there is still so much of it to come."

"Give in to the fear." Smoky tendrils formed the outline of a black unicorn in front of Eiryenne. Their voices deepened and seemed to come from its mouth. "Give us your soul. We can read your mind, there is nowhere to hide."

"Correction. You can read her *emotions*." A new voice rang out through the darkness. A deep voice, melodious and filled with the underlying echo of a rumble, like the roar of a thousand fires. "*Raikuro!*"

There was a blazing, blinding flash. And the darkness melted away. Eiryenne blinked a couple of times as her eyes took in her new surroundings. She was standing in the centre of a large room with a high ceiling and crumbling ruins surrounding a central dais. On it stood the sirens.

All of Eiryenne's companions were here, too, lying at the foot of the dais and blinking in the new light.

She turned to see the dragon mages striding across the room, fire blazing from their hands and chasing the last of the sirens' magic away.

The sirens were looking at them with disgust.

"There," screeched the blonde one. "Intruders! Abominations! What … what *are* you?"

Lianos gave Eiryenne a hand up before checking the unconscious leopard. "Funny things, sirens," he said. "They control males through song. Females they usually kill or coerce because they can read their emotions, which is different from reading minds, mind you. They can tell what you're feeling, not what you're thinking; not the same thing, technically."

"Are the others going to be okay?" Eiryenne asked, pointing to the girls lying by the dais.

Lianos nodded. "They're fine. The whole thing was just an illusion. Sirens are good at those."

Eiryenne looked over at Tina, still unconscious. She hadn't really drowned. She just thought she had.

"Why cannot we control them?" demanded the siren. "They appear male."

"Face only," Danzi tapped his beard. "The mind is not limited by gender. The mind is dragon."

"Y–you should not exist," stammered the blonde siren. "You–you cannot exist!"

"No, we *will* control you," shouted the other. "We control all. All men are powerless before us. We control your desires, your thoughts, your emotions."

Lianos frowned. "Aren't you listening to what he's telling you?"

"No. No one is immune."

"You're wrong," growled Danzi. He looked at the sirens with merciless draconic eyes, his gaze settling on the face of the dark-haired one on the left. He'd seen her before, and she annoyed him just as much as she had the first time.

He began to walk up the dais with slow, purposeful steps. A predator's stalk. "I feel no lust but for blood, no desire but that for power, and no love but for killing," he snarled. "You have no power over *me*, siren." He drew his broadsword, gleaming with steel and blood and gold.

The sirens drew back, screeching.

Danzi's eyes flashed malevolently, his lips curled in a feral snarl. The molten spring of rage in his chest had been tapped, and his fury spilled out into his eyes like wildfire. These pathetic creatures were utterly disgusting. They represented everything he hated about the *pyerams*—the lowly species they so desperately controlled.

He stopped, hefting his blade up high. "You say you can read emotions. So read mine, siren, and despair."

The siren stumbled back as fear poured into her face. "So much rage. A heart filled with unimaginable hatred. Fuelled by vengeance and sadism. The fire to kill, blinding you, driving you, making you unstoppable. Wait, the dragon. I remember—"

"*Die, you lowly Okorosagen,*" he hissed, driving his sword into the siren's torso, halfway up to the hilt. She gasped with pain as the sharp blade sliced right through her and her blood began to pour out onto it, turning the blade crimson.

There was an evil smirk on Danzi's face. He wrenched the hilt cruelly in the siren's belly, making her give a sharp groan as more blood spewed out to splatter onto his sleeves. For a few long moments he simply watched her writhe in pain. But it wouldn't take her long to bleed to death, and he wanted the finishing blow to be a hack of his cold steel blade rather than just simple blood loss. With a final sharp twist he sliced horizontally through the siren's chest, her body falling to the ground with a satisfying thud, landing in a pool of her own blood.

"Just a *little* overkill, no?" Lianos said casually, cocking his head. "Or have you two met before?"

"We have." Danzi frowned. "You try being trapped at the bottom of a siren-crazed pile of demons. See how you like that."

The second siren backed away. "Could I tempt you with their deaths?" she asked. "Anyone in the Resistance—"

The dragon mage looked thoughtful. Restructure the Resistance? Then again, there wasn't that much to cut out in the first place.

But then Lianos jumped up to the dais. "Now that's where I come in." He lopped off the siren's head with one of his knives. It was a clean cut, and the head fell to the floor with a light clunk. "We need every man and woman that the Resistance has," he said. "Especially considering recent events."

Beside the dais, the siren's victims were starting to grow more aware of their surroundings. Cassandra was sitting up, her hands over her mouth.

"Oh my god," she squeaked. "You just chopped off that woman's head."

Lianos shrugged, wiping the blood off his knife. "The *siren's* head. It was necessary. The only way to break the power they had over the camp's men."

"Better than what the first one had to go through," Taymel added, shuddering.

Cassandra still looked shaken. Her cheeks were pale, and her hands shook. "But she was a *woman*. And she was pretty. You should have been nice to her."

Therein lay the difference between dragons and other species. "Wrong," Danzi said. "We have no concept of beauty or gender. So, what if individuals within a species have slightly different shapes? Individuals of different species are different shapes, too. It makes no difference to us. Regardless of species, regardless of gender, all we see," he bent down to scoop up a handful of twigs, which were scattered across the dais, along with leaves and petals as though part of some ritual, "are entities with blood to be spilled and wills to be broken." He held two twigs between his thumb and forefinger. One of the twigs was thick and sturdy, the other was thin and brittle. "Some," he squeezed, and the smaller twig cracked, "just break more easily than others." But he continued squeezing, and soon the thicker twig, too, snapped.

In a flash of blinding fire, he shifted to his true form. He'd only taken the human one to spite the sirens as they killed them, to have them killed by something wearing the shape of that which they supposedly controlled. The ultimate disgrace. Now the red dragon stood quietly at the edge of the dais, his scales darkened by the dimness of the lighting. At his side, Lianos, too, transformed. He stepped over the siren's body and stopped next to his brother.

"Come, brother," Danzi said.

Lianos's eyes widened slightly as all his scales steeled themselves to hide a shudder.

"We are finished here." Danzi opened his mouth, and a jet of fire exploded from his jaws, blowing a hole in the side of the building; the one they'd arrived through had already sealed itself off.

Lianos lowered his head. He looked pensive. Whatever he'd been expecting Danzi to say, that had not been it. The beginning of his phrase, however, had brought about some memories he'd prefer stay forgotten.

With a light sigh, he launched himself into the air and followed Danzi through the hole. Once outside, however, he paused to turn and pour more fire into the hole, extending it down to the floor so that the girls could get out.

Cassandra was still shivering, looking at where the dragons had disappeared into the sky. "They're so ... so—"

"Not human?" Eiryenne filled in.

***

Clean-up at the camp was well underway. With the sirens' death, the men regained their wills, and the task of putting everything back together began. The entire place was a mess: tents and cabins in ruins, debris scattered everywhere, and the combat arena a blackened shamble.

Mels had been found dead with Leo's arrow in her side. One of the councillors had been burned to death, another had been trampled by Ha the minotaur, and a cook had been speared by Tukse. But overall, there were surprisingly few deaths, though the range of injuries was great, and healers like Eiryenne were kept very busy for the next while.

"What I *still* don't get," Yolen said, "is how they found the camp in the first place."

He stood on the top floor of the formerly hidden temple, now unearthed, discussing things with the dragons and Riard during a break in the clean-up.

Riard pursed his lips. He was flustered. Their emergency Council meeting had yielded nothing, and he didn't know what to do any more. First the news of the army's fall, and now this siren madness.

He couldn't tell the other councillors the entire truth, and he wasn't sure whether they should move the camp immediately. And even if they did move it, to where? Where would they be safe now that there was no army to defend them?

Eiryenne's footsteps echoed loudly on the stone steps. She was coming upstairs to tell Riard they'd run out of Tebrew potion, the best for burns, and ask him how to brew some more when she saw the group gathered in an alcove. From their expressions she judged that the potion was probably the least of their worries right now, so she settled against the wall of reddish black stone to wait. It was well into the night, and darkness had long since settled over the temple. To her human eyes, the others were barely visible in the light of a fire burning in a brazier.

"I don't know," Riard muttered. "We got all the scouts and moon kirin during the day. Danzi, are you *sure* you weren't followed when you flew back to camp?"

The red dragon's scales rustled against the rock as his horns glinted in the shadows cast by the wall. "Quite sure. I told you, I came across a patrol, but I made short work of them. There was no one else in the area."

Yolen frowned. "Perhaps we missed a scout? Or Varcroft's had his eye on this place for longer than we knew?"

"We'd know," Danzi reminded him. "We have his records."

"He could've gotten the information from someone in the field. We've still got operatives out there. Or perhaps some kind of tracking enchantment."

Yolen continued to talk, but his voice began to drift over Eiryenne's head. She was thinking.

"Danzi," she said slowly, looking thoughtful. "You said you came across a patrol on the way here, right? And you said that you ... that you had him for lunch."

The dragon nodded.

"Um, I was just thinking ...the sirens were in the area, obviously, but you couldn't hear them. What if you ate an anchor?"

The dragon raised an eyebrow. "What are you trying to say?"

Riard and Yolen fell silent.

Lianos blinked.

"Could they track that?" Riard asked, frowning.

"I don't know much about siren magic," the dragon said with a shrug. "But I do know that they need a live mind to serve as a host."

"Well, did you eat him alive?"

"That is irrelevant. Nothing would survive in my gut for long."

"How did you bite him?" Yolen asked.

"Er, let's see." Danzi mimed a bit with his jaws. "Just one bite across the body and two for the last one. He was fat."

"Was he wearing a helmet?"

"Yeah. A crunchy one."

Riard kneaded his forehead. "If it was Erythdium metal, that would have preserved the signal for a little while longer. They're standard issue for southern patrols."

Danzi frowned. "I don't like what you're saying."

But Yolen confirmed it by scanning him with his magic and sensing a tiny piece of metal in his stomach, with the faintest echo of siren magic.

"Well, it looks like we've found our loophole. How ironic." The mage sighed. "Danzi, did you *really* have to eat him? You led the sirens here." Riard sounded beyond exasperated.

"Well, how was I supposed to know?" demanded the dragon. He hadn't been able to stop to hunt on the way back from Tartaway. He'd been hungry. "I've eaten loads of people, and until now not one has ever been a problem after going down my throat." He paused. "Besides, I fixed the situation, did I not?"

"Yes, the same way that you *fix* everything else," Riard burst out. It seemed that the horror and indignation he'd been holding back ever since finding out about Hurraine's army was surfacing at last.

"In all fairness," Yolen added. "It wasn't his fault."

Riard shook his head darkly. "It never is. It … ugh." He paused, looking up at the red dragon. "You know what? I have quite enough on my plate now, largely thanks to you, Danzi Daggoras. The camp is a mess. The Council has no idea that our only army is demolished, that all our brave soldiers are dead and that we need to move the camp immediately. Why I'm still not telling them, I have no idea. The truth is, I don't know what to do. I don't know if this camp is safe. I have no idea whether we'll all be struck down tomorrow, massacred like pigs, just like our brothers on Fetlo. And if we move the camp, I'm starting to think we won't be relocating any more. We'll be running. In all honesty, it is starting to dawn on me that the Resistance is finished."

He was breathless by the end of his speech, now looking forlornly at Danzi.

Eiryenne raised her eyebrows. She'd never seen Riard lose control like that. But something told her that Yolen shared his sentiment; the elf studied the ground at his feet darkly, his self control greater than Riard's, but not by much.

"Unless you have any better ideas about the situation?" he said.

Danzi sighed, his wings rolling up and down with the motion of his shoulders. "Look, I'll—"

"Don't you think that you've done enough?" Riard told him pointedly. He slumped against the wall and looked away.

"I'll be out of your way soon enough. Come four more days," Danzi said. "And the next step of my plan—"

"What happens in four days?" asked Yolen.

Danzi shifted to his human form and took Varcroft's scrolls from his pocket, flipping to a certain page and laying it out on an engraved, table-like rocky shelf projecting from the temple's floor. "This," he said, pointing triumphantly to the parchment. "This is the supply caravan that moves out in four days. I'll hit is as soon as it comes around Macharond Pass. Combined with attacks on the Rento and Yuanjuz carriers." He continued on, the fire back in his eyes as he outlined his plan.

But Yolen still looked gloomy. "Danzi," he began. "This plan would work brilliantly, but it assumes that you've got a Resistance leader and his army on your side fighting those battles and whittling the Emperor's forces down from the front. By yourself, the most you'll do is inconvenience him. The other hits will never work. I don't care if you're the most powerful mage in the world, a war is not won by a single warrior when you face an empire of millions."

The dragon mage faltered and fell silent, darkness filling his gaze and weighing down his heart. The problem was that Riard was right. He just didn't want to think about it. He didn't want to confront this issue and admit that it was his own as well.

The truth was they didn't stand a chance. What had once been Golenhar's army, painstakingly brought up from the edges of the Empire, and then his own, was now nothing. And without the army, they were sitting ducks. All they could do was run and hide.

Danzi gritted his teeth. He could have flown away from all this any time he chose. There was a reason he didn't. He was too stubborn to admit defeat, even when it stared him in the face. Even when it meant he'd most likely die fighting a never-ending, impossible war. Even if he always brought doom to the very force he had tried so hard to bring to victory.

Lianos interrupted his thoughts. He'd been silent so far in the conversation, but now he looked at Danzi with thoughtful, soul-searching eyes. "Well, not the exactly the first time you've found yourself in this kind of situation." He switched to Draconic. "*Don't you wonder why Riard remains loyal? Why they're all gathered here, in what could be their darkest hour, venting their gripes to you? Old habits die hard, you said it yourself. You've proven yourself in impossible circumstances before. And even if they don't know it, they're looking to you to do something.*"

Danzi frowned. *"That time is gone."* But as he looked back at Riard and Yolen, he realized that he did see the desperation in their gazes. And that searching look, as if they were waiting, as if they wanted something.

Yolen glanced at Lianos. Then he looked at the floor. "Take command," he said abruptly.

"What?" The dragon mage's mouth sagged slightly with surprise.

"You heard me. Hurraine's gone. We're stuck. That gives you an opportunity." He paused. "You've done great things before, Danzi Daggoras. Perhaps we need you at the helm again."

Slowly, Danzi shook his head. "No. My days as the leader of anything are long over. Riard is right; I have done enough damage here. Salvage what you have left and run. It's all you can do."

"Giving up?" Lianos said, sounding surprised. "That is so unlike you."

Danzi looked morose. "I'm not giving up. What is there to give up but that which is already lost?" he growled, sounding more cross by the second.

Eiryenne frowned. This was the last place she expected to find apathy. Danzi always seemed to have a solution for something, to pull an impossible trick out for any problem he encountered. And yet here he was, openly admitting they'd lost. He wasn't even going to try.

She stepped toward the dragon mage until she was looking him square in the face. Beneath his forlorn, apathetic mask there was something else.

"You're afraid," she said quietly.

With a growl, Danzi rounded on her, smashing his fist into the red-black rock above her head, his eyes flashing. Eiryenne flinched, and terror made her heart race, but she didn't back away. She balled her shaking hands into fists.

"You're afraid of failure," she finished.

Danzi stared at her with smouldering eyes.

"I think we all are," Lianos said quietly. "Because we know all too well what failure brings." He looked around at them. Best to defuse the situation before it got out of hand. "Now, why don't we all go downstairs? I'll make you all some tea." He put a hand on Riard's shoulder.

The mage nodded. "That sounds good."

His brother didn't reply. He turned away from them, shifting into his dragon form and taking flight.

12 ~ His Vision

A little while after leaving Riard and Yolen with steaming mugs of his best tea and giving Eiryenne a quick lift back to their makeshift healing tent, Lianos flew over the camp to join the red dragon on the peak of the temple hill.

The darkness didn't hinder Lianos's eyes; the only thing it took from his vision was colour, not clarity. Danzi's scales were darkened to a deep, dark greyish brown with only a few reddish undertones where the starlight lit them, like embers of a dying fire.

The blue dragon hooked his claws into the rock and clambered up to sit next to him.

"I think he was on to something, you know," he said casually. "You, taking over again."

Danzi shook his head. "I am a failure and an outcast. Who in their right mind would want me to have the chance to ruin this force *twice*?" he said bitterly.

"I do," Lianos said easily. "And so does Yolen. And Riard. Eiryenne and Leo, too. The rest just need a bit of convincing."

"Who can I possibly convince, and how?" Danzi asked in a sunken, hollow voice. "They don't believe in me anymore. Quite rightly, too."

"You should start with yourself. If you don't want it, it's definitely not going to happen," the blue dragon said more firmly. "You need to get yourself out of that self-defeating mindset and recognize that you were once a great military leader. All those qualities are still there, buried beneath your bitterness. Learn from your mistakes, and you could be unstoppable."

Danzi opened his mouth to say something, then closed it again. He still looked grim.

"Let me just say this," Lianos said. "I've seen you build up an army from scratch once. And I believe that you could do it again."

"That was different," Danzi protested. "I was—"

"Motivated. Very, motivated."

"I was going to say mad."

"Well, that too. But the facts stand—you still managed to win." Lianos spread his wings and took off into the night, leaving the other dragon to his thoughts.

***

Eiryenne wrapped up her round in the healing tent and stepped outside. A million thoughts and questions burned in her mind. From the fate of the Resistance to the camp's safety and Danzi's controversial stance, the weight of it all seemed to press down on her shoulders as the topics whirled in her head all at once.

Were they safe? What would happen to the Resistance? Was it a war even worth fighting?

She gave Leo a quiet nod as she passed him. He met her gaze but didn't say anything. He'd been rather quiet since he found out that he'd killed Mels, even though it hadn't been his fault. Seeing his light face so troubled, she didn't have the heart to tell him the extent of the situation and all that had gone on at Temple Hill that night.

Eiryenne was tired after the most intensive night of healing she'd ever done. From cuts to burns to enchantments, there had been a lot of things to deal with. She'd spent every last drop of her magic and any that she borrowed from other mages or storage stones. Physically, she was exhausted, but her mind was too restless to let her turn in for the night just yet.

She wandered around to the southern end of the hill. Since the meal tent had been destroyed, the surviving cooks had switched to one of the old fort-houses to serve dinner. It was two storeys high and made of old, antique stone. Just like the temple, these buildings had been here when the camp was built, and they'd been converted into forts for use in case of siege, though at the moment the southern one was being used to serve food and drinks. And since most of the exhausted kids had gone to bed, the place was more of an open bar. The tables had been slid to the side and along a long, narrow counter, one of the cooks was pouring a glass of ale for Yolen, who was quietly chatting with one of the other elves.

Then Danzi strode in, making his way through the shadows and walking up to the counter with something less than his usual confident manner.

"A pint of Dusk," he said to the second cook behind the counter, pointing to a bottle filled to the brim with a golden liqueur.

"Diluted with what?" asked the cook.

"Not diluted."

"All right," the man replied, chuckling. He took the bottle and put it in front of Danzi. "Though how you can even stand something like that I don't know. It burns most mouths, but then dragons breathe fire, so perhaps it's no wonder."

The dragon mage scooped up the bottle in one hand and an empty tankard in the other. He turned to go up the stairs.

In the dark, Eiryenne sensed, rather than saw, Lianos walking by her. He stopped at her side.

"Can't sleep?"

She shook her head.

"Don't blame you."

"It's just, I mean, what are we going to do?" she said.

Lianos put a hand on her shoulder. "We'll figure it out. We always do."

"And Danzi, can he really—" she began.

"Why don't you ask him yourself?" he suggested. "If you want to talk to him, now would be a good time. Four cups will loosen his tongue. Don't believe most of what he says after seven, though. After that, it would be wise to step away. And if he got to ten, you wouldn't want to be in the same building as him."

"I've never seen him do ten," remarked Yolen, who was making his way back from the bar.

"I have," Lianos said. "It wasn't pretty."

Eiryenne hesitated. On one hand, she did not want to end up facing whatever Danzi was like when he drank too much. On the other, she had a small window of opportunity to ask him whatever she wanted to. And she had to admit that there were a lot of things she wanted to talk to him about. "I didn't think alcohol had an effect on dragons," she mused. "I mean, I've seen you drinking ale in the Empire, and it didn't seem to do anything."

"It doesn't work too well on us, no," Lianos said. "We burn through it too quickly. That's why he needs that really concentrated stuff to feel its effects. If you ever had any unanswered questions, the time to ask them is now. Otherwise, make peace with the silence. Most of the time, that's all he'll give you."

Eiryenne took a breath. Then she folded her hands behind her back and resolutely marched through the bar and up the stairs.

The balcony curved around the upper level of the building. It looked out away from the hill and the camp, across the fields where the horses grazed, and the forests rustled off in the distance.

Danzi didn't seem to notice her approach. He was leaning on the railing, looking out over the moors. There was no light save that of the quarter moon, already well into its nightly trek across the sky. Around it, glimpses of stars sometimes shone through clear patches, but most of the sky was covered by a velvety layer of grey clouds. Banks of fog gathered around the trees and floated in the hollows within the swaying fields of grass. Everything was cast in a shade of grey or dark blue, the colours muted by the darkness.

There were coiled, curling spires of rock coming up from the lower ledge of the balcony that joined the wide, flat piece that was the top of the railing. The rock was worn and steel grey, cracks snaking across its surface in some places. It mirrored the look of the rest of the fort—a place that might have been fancy and prominent many years ago, but it had long since fallen into ruin.

The bottle of golden liquor stood on the ledge, its yellow depths dimmed and glimmering with silver instead. Danzi raised the heavy glass tankard to his lips, his eyes distant. He looked worn-out and tired.

When Eiryenne first met him, she'd thought he had the air of someone who'd done things. Now he looked like someone who'd done too much. Seen too much.

Slowly, she went to the balcony. Now that Danzi was in front of her, she wasn't sure where to begin.

"So," she talked when she judged him to be almost at the end of his fourth drink, "you led the Resistance once."

He nodded sadly.

"What-what happened?"

Danzi took another long sip from his tankard. "It was my fault," he said gloomily. "I led them into a trap. Just like the one Hurraine walked into last week. I doomed them all, and I didn't even know it."

"But I also heard that there could have been spies involved—"

Danzi laughed harshly. "Blackthorn? I wish I could pin it all on him, I really do. Certainly, he betrayed our plans and contributed to my downfall. But the biggest fault there that day was mine. If I hadn't brought them through Kyrahgrun Pass, if I hadn't been so arrogant and so, so *stupid*, they'd be alive. And we'd still have a territory extending out past Fetlo. That wouldn't have had to happen. Hell, we might even be at the capital by now, but I had to lose it all. I can't let that happen again. Not ever." He took another swig and finished his tankard before reaching for the bottle to pour himself another glass.

"But doesn't that mean giving up on everything that the Resistance ever stood for? Don't you believe in that anymore?" Eiryenne asked.

He scoffed. "Of course I do," he said. "You'll be hard-pressed to find someone who is more against Varcroft's theft of personal freedom, his oppression of free will, and the endless warring that his reign of blood brings. Because I know what it's like to not have any of that for such a long time .... It's funny. I had so much blood on my hands even before I joined the Resistance. I thought I could make up for all those things I'd done. Turn my life in a different direction. Fight for something meaningful. But I only ended up leaving with even more lives taken, thanks to me. Not directly, like before, but still, the lives of all those thousands who died, even more innocent blood on my hands. It's ironic." He finished his fifth cup and poured another.

Eiryenne was silent for a moment. With one secret down, it appeared she'd found another. She understood what he said about Kyrahgrun, but his remarks about his previous deeds made her head spin. "What were your reasons for joining the Resistance in the first place, then? Wouldn't they still stand?"

Danzi put his tankard down, placing both hands on the stone and straightening. He looked out across the misty fields with a glint of old pride and ancient determination in his distant eyes. He seemed to think back for a second, his sombre cloak lifting and his gaze clearing.

"When you look at the world," he said, "and you don't like what you see, you decide to make a change in it."

His words hung in the air as if they cast new life into the fog that began to trickle down toward the fort.

Danzi cleared his sixth tankard and wiped his mouth on his sleeve before continuing. He gazed wistfully up at the clouds. "My vision is to see *all of Shotang* united under one crown. And not Varcroft's, mind you." He paused. "And Remfuria, too, for that matter. I owe that country a lot."

Eiryenne blinked. "What's Remfuria got to do with all this?" As far as she knew, the Emperor's reach didn't go quite that far. "Don't tell me Varcroft has a base there."

"It doesn't have anything to do with Varcroft," Danzi said slowly. "It has to do with me."

"How?"

Danzi's face darkened. "Not even this," he tapped the tankard, "is enough to make me divulge what most mars my conscience. At least not yet. And think about it, do you truly wish to know the depths of my darkness?" He looked at her for a long moment, his face half-covered by shadows. He couldn't look less human if he tried. Then he poured himself another drink.

Eiryenne blinked. He was at seven already. Her window of opportunity was closing fast. "Why won't you lead us?" she said softly. "We need your help."

Danzi drank half the tankard in one go. "Haven't you been *listening*?" he said with a frown. "I can't do it. I'll fail again, and we'll all die. Best for me to back off and let you die separately. Then I can fly around in circles and pretend to be doing something with whatever time I have left so that *when* Varcroft finally gets me, I can pretend that I've done something meaningful. Don't you see how pointless it all is?" He polished off the last of his liquor and went to pour more of it from the bottle, but the liquid sloshed past his cup and splashed onto the boards at his feet. Tossing the tankard to the side, where it landed on the stone tiles and shattered, Danzi took up the bottle itself instead and drank from it directly, the yellow liquid sloshing all over his face in the process.

Eiryenne frowned. She knew that she should go now, but she couldn't help saying one more thing. "You're so afraid that you won't even try. You've given up on this battle before it could really begin."

"Indeed," he slurred. "If I'm already beaten, why bother?"

"Unless you're not," she said, not sure how much of her speech was registering with him but deciding to keep talking anyway. "Unless you just *think* you are. What if you can make this work? What if you can actually *win* this?"

"That would be the day," he muttered. Then he smiled. "Such optimism. You know, you remind me of Freya sometimes, just a little."

"Who's Freya?" Eiryenne asked. She remembered hearing the name before somewhere but couldn't remember exactly where.

"She was my friend. My best friend." Danzi trailed off, bringing the bottle to his lips. "Gone now. If I hadn't been so ignorant." He growled, smashing his fist into the rock. Fire began to glow around his hand. "But I made him pay. I *always* make them pay. Who now dares to face Daggoras in guilt?"

A hand reached out of the shadows to snatch the bottle out of his grip. Eiryenne turned to see Lianos standing there, looking concerned.

"Now, that's quite enough," he said firmly.

"Give it back." Danzi's words were hard to make out now, but the frown was deepening.

"Okay, just stay calm." Eiryenne saw Lianos quickly switch the bottles behind his back and hand a different one to Danzi. His brother didn't seem to notice the difference, his senses were too dulled. He brought it to his lips and drank about half, then collapsed against the railing.

"What's in there?" Eiryenne whispered.

"Regular water mixed with some sleeping potion," Lianos whispered back. "He'll be out in a few minutes." He turned to the drunk dragon mage. "Now, I know you probably won't remember this tomorrow," Lianos said. He bent over Danzi. "But I also know it's probably the only time I'll get away with saying it." He paused. "A wise person once told me ... all right, *you* once told me that a leader had to forego his own biases and make decisions for the good of the people. But these days you've been consumed by your own biases, no? So much so that you've forgotten your own lessons." He paused and lowered his voice, but his tone was more forceful, more laced with fire than Eiryenne had ever heard. "A hundred years of darkness forged a will of iron, you claimed. A spirit that could never be broken. Don't tell me you survived all that only to perish from your own guilty doubts."

Danzi made a noise that sounded like a breathy, rattling echo of a growl. He struggled for a few seconds but was too incapacitated to get up.

Lianos stood back and turned away. He gestured to Eiryenne, and they walked back downstairs.

The combined effect of the alcohol and potion quickly turned Danzi's thoughts into a fuzzy, incoherent soup of blurriness. His head fell forward onto his chest as his consciousness started to fade.

Downstairs, a pair of drunk elves were laughing and joking with a half-conscious Molekk.

"Madness, isn't it?" shouted Leo's uncle. "I didn't believe half the reports, do you? Take Bursair, for instance. Last week he claimed to have been chased across the northern tundra by a horde of angry ice kirin before almost being trampled to death by a team of griffins, all led by this black Pegasus."

***

The black Pegasus swooped down over him, bashing him in the head with his hooves. Danzi roared and transformed, leaping into the air after him. He seized the hapless pegasus in his jaws and shook his head. But Blackthorn seemed to be made of liquid metal; Danzi's teeth did not pierce his hide, and as soon as the pressure was lifted, Blackthorn's neck flowed back together to its original, unsquashed state.

He grinned maliciously. "Still can't get rid of me, can you?"

Then he blasted Danzi with his magic, sending the dragon falling out of the sky. Danzi suddenly found himself back in human form, still falling, into blackness that seemed to try to rise up and consume him. Its dark tendrils pulled him into the heart of a deep, dark grotto—the heart of a long-extinct volcano.

Danzi landed hard, winded, and broken. He struggled to his feet as Blackthorn materialized in front of him, now in human form as well.

The fire mage tried to shoot flames from his hands, but no fire leapt from his fingers. His magic was gone.

Blackthorn sent another bolt of light through Danzi, who convulsed in pain.

His hand went to his belt, but his sword wasn't there; neither was Golenhar's dagger. So Danzi just shifted to his other knee and leapt at Blackthorn empty-handed, punching him in the face as hard as he could.

"Why—won't—you- just—die," Danzi snarled with a mixture of rage and desperation as he punched him over and over, but even though the force of each blow should have been enough to shatter bone or even rock, they glanced off Blackthorn as if they held no power whatsoever.

No matter how hard he hit, he couldn't do any damage. He couldn't wipe that infuriating smirk off Blackthorn's face.

The Pegasus mage grabbed Danzi by the throat and, lifting him off his feet, smashed his head into the wall of black rock so hard that he saw stars.

Danzi's hands went to his pockets, searching for something, anything that he could use. But the various knives and gems he'd kept were nowhere to be seen.

Then he felt something hard against his fingertip. He grabbed it and pulled it out of his jacket.

The unicorn horn.

Danzi gripped the horn firmly at its base and swung his arm over his head, plunging it into Blackthorn's chest. To his surprise, it sank in easily, and reddish-black blood began to trickle across its pearly white surface. He yanked the horn out in a shower of fresh blood.

Blackthorn looked taken aback. He let go of Danzi as one hand went to his wound to try to stop the blood flow.

Danzi didn't think, he just reacted. His arm snapped forward again as he drove the horn into Blackthorn's torso once more. With a satisfying *squelch*, it bit deep into his chest.

The Pegasus mage drew back, coughing up blood, but Danzi seized his shoulder with his free hand and held the struggling man still while he continued to stab him, over and over. Blackthorn shape-shifted a few times between stabs, but nothing could stop Danzi now. He was delirious with bloodlust and so caught up in the moment that he continued to stab the Pegasus mage long after he stopped breathing.

The sound of footsteps made him pause. Panting, Danzi stood back, the battered body at his feet, the dripping horn in his hand and a mad gleam in his eye. Red splatters covered his arms. He turned, the horn still dripping with blood, to see a light-haired woman dressed in blue walking toward him. Her expression was saddened and disappointed as she studied the blood on Danzi's hands.

"So much blood," she whispered. "Hasn't there been enough?"

"You can't change who I am," Danzi said quietly.

"*You* can," she replied. "I've seen you make quite the turnaround already. And I know you're still capable of it. Or is this all that your life is about now—killing people from your past that have crossed you in some way?"

Danzi shook his head and looked at the horn, dripping with the pegasus's blood. "It's good enough for me," he said. "Besides, Blackthorn *killed* you. Wouldn't you, of all people, want him dead?"

"Danzi, are you so caught up in your own rage that you forget I never had the heart for revenge?" Freya took a step closer.

"Wait, you're dead, " he said, shaking his head and trying to clear it. Then he shrugged. "I must be dreaming. You're just a figment of my imagination."

"Not quite," she said. She reached down and took Danzi's hand, which was at his side and still wrapped around the horn. Freya lifted it up in front of them. "My spirit is connected to this. You know that Tairung visited Eiryenne in her dreams. Thanks to this, I can drop in on yours. Not as often as I'd like," she paused. "But it's me."

Danzi was silent, observing her face more carefully. Then he looked down at their hands, her fingers spotless and his bloody, entwined on the unicorn's horn.

"This," Freya shook the bloody horn gently, "is not what that is for." A wave of blue light rose from her fingers and washed over the horn. The blood on it and on Danzi disappeared.

With a start, he realized that he could feel her magic. Danzi raised his eyebrows. "It's you," he said softly. "It's really your spirit,"

Freya reached out, and he let her pull him into her embrace, wrapping his arms around her in return. She felt warm and alive, but when he looked closer, he saw that the magic beneath her skin didn't flow, and the blood in her veins was stationary. Her heart was not beating.

"It's good to see you," he whispered.

"It's good to see you, too," she replied. Freya gave him a gentle squeeze then drew back enough so that she could look him closely in the face. "You're at war with the world, Danzi."

"Well, maybe the world is at war with me," he retorted.

"You can't go on like this," she said. "You've stirred up a lot of trouble everywhere. Neither the Emperor nor the Resistance is happy with you. One of them is going to eventually kill you if you don't choose another path."

"I've survived for decades as a fugitive," he retorted with a shrug. "I can manage."

"With how many close calls?" she pointed out. "You didn't tell the others about how the traps in the capital almost killed you, or that the igarevin spear was inches away from your heart, or, well, you get the point. After all, you travel alone when you can't heal your own wounds."

"Trust me, Freya, I can take a lot of damage," Danzi said darkly.

"Maybe so. But everything has its limits. So do you." She paused. "You are powerful, but you also have powerful enemies. You can't do this alone. You need allies. You need a good, strong army at your back before you can take down Varcroft."

Danzi dipped his head. "I'll think about it."

"Now, it's time for you to wake. Wake to a new beginning, my friend. And triumph."

***

Eiryenne wandered slowly down the path, still half-asleep. She'd slept in quite a bit after spending most of the night working and healing. But she was still tired. Maybe a cup of Lianos's tea would fix that.

It was strange, surreal almost, to see the destruction in daylight. As if seeing it all by the light of the sun cemented the connection between what could have been a nightmare and this new day. There were still wrecked tents and cabins, with scattered bricks and torn planks of wood scattered in the soot and dirt. But they looked different in the sun. Gone were the dark undertones of red and black and the shadows clinging to every object's underside. The bright white sunlight shone hard against pale wooden fibres, which reflected something of the bright greyish blue expanse of the sky. The entire colour palette changed to bright, barely saturated blues and grays. The edges of the still-standing cabins had a hard white border from where the light behind them hit the thin layer of dew draped along their wooden frames by the fog in the night.

A cool breeze of crisp, fresh morning air blew away the scents of burned wood and upturned earth, replacing it with the scents of dew and leaves.

The door to Lianos's cabin was open, sunlight streaming through it to play out muted patterns on the scraped tile floor. Eiryenne walked through.

Lianos was sitting at his window.

"Good morning," Eiryenne said.

He nodded to her but put a finger to his lips. Then he gestured to the centre of the room.

There stood Danzi, leaning over the table, his brow wrinkled with concentration. His cloak and sword still hung on the pegs on the wall where he'd left them the day before. He didn't look nearly as hung-over as could be expected. Instead, he was practically brimming with a new, fiery energy.

He was looking at a map of the Empire.

"The thing is, all possibilities, even the remote ones, are within the borders," he said to no one in particular. "Obviously, that's where I'll end up going, but it would be good to have something closer by, first. Though there's hardly anyone beyond the Empire we could seek out … elves, Dyre wolves, ogres, they all live inside the Empire."

"What about humans?" Eiryenne suggested. She peered at the tangled network of small southern nations around the camp. "There's got to be some countries out here just as fed up with Varcroft as we are."

Danzi frowned. "Humans," he muttered.

"What?" Eiryenne retorted. "You can't count us out completely. If there's no one else out here, you might as well start with us."

Lianos raised an eyebrow.

"What good are humans?" Danzi said. "We need mages and monsters."

"Okay, well, *in theory.*" Eiryenne walked over to the table so that she could see the map. "In theory, if you were looking for non-magical allies, where would you look?"

Danzi looked back at the map. She had a point; he was letting his own biases get in his way again. That was the wrong thing to do.

"Well, in theory …," he trailed his finger along the network of countries before coming to a stop on a small, outlined patch, located to the north of the camp, and sharing a border with the Empire. "Here. Rudengard. It's a small human kingdom on the Empire's edge. You can imagine the problems with a neighbour like that. Varcroft's been invading them for years now. He's usually just too preoccupied elsewhere ever to finish the job."

"But we got a report this morning that he's moving in again," Lianos added. "With the Resistance out of the way, I guess he thinks there's nothing to stop him."

"Does he, now?" Danzi looked at the map more closely. There was a new glint in his eye today. A fresh determination underlying his words. Nothing like the broken wreck he'd been last night. "We shall see."

Lianos came over to stand across the table from Danzi. "So, what's the plan?"

"I can fly to Rudengard easily enough. It's not that far. From there I'll fly to the border, then cross the mountain chain to reach Ilteravande. There might still be a few people there who'll listen to me. And then," he added some notes in Draconic to various places on the map, drawing circles and adding symbols, "it begins."

"So how soon do you expect to finish the war?" Eiryenne asked naively.

Danzi laughed. "It's a process. We need to rebuild our army, find allies, spread word of revolution. Tip the scales. And, when the scales are tipped far enough … strike."

"What makes you think Rudengard's king will listen to you?" Lianos asked. "They don't like non-humans. And you're not exactly the most easy-going individual. This kind of thing calls for diplomacy."

"You're right," Danzi nodded. "Someone like Riard would come in handy. And Yolen to talk to the elves."

"I don't know how well-received Yolen would be in his hometown," Lianos pointed out. "As for Riard, well, you'll have a hard time slipping him out from under the Council's nose. They won't approve it, and he won't go against them again."

"What about you?"

Lianos looked away. "New orders, unfortunately. Came this morning while you were still sleeping it off. Molekk's sending me out this afternoon to head to Fetlo to see what I can find. From there it's on to check our operatives in the east and whatever else they can think of. You know how it goes." His jaw tensed as he looked back up at Danzi, but the other dragon mage merely shrugged.

"Very well." Danzi went silent, staring at the map again.

Eiryenne was still examining it as well, tracing the routes with her index finger. So, this was it. Danzi was finally springing into action. He was going to go and start a revolution. She was hopeful and doubtful at the same time, but there was something inherently exciting about the notion as well.

"Can I go?" she said abruptly.

Both of them looked at her in surprise.

"You? Seriously?" Danzi said in disbelief.

She herself could hardly believe what she'd said. But she nodded. "Yeah. I mean, I think having someone human to talk to the king will help. And," she paused, "I guess I've realized that I just want to be out there, part of it. It's better than sitting in camp and waiting to be slaughtered." *Yeah, great idea,* she thought. *Instead of waiting for trouble, I'm going to go find it.* She gulped, suddenly not so sure.

"I think that's a good idea," Lianos said. "It takes more than a sword to win people's trust. You won't convince any of the other adult warriors to go and your allies are all bound by their other orders." He paused. "The people you want to talk to in Ilteravande … Yolen's parents, right?"

Danzi nodded.

"Why don't you take Leo? That'll get their attention for sure," he continued.

"Two kids?"

"Not just two kids. Leo and Eiryenne. Two up-and-coming young warriors, ready and willing to serve your cause. Plus, they could really use the field experience, I think."

Danzi looked thoughtful. "Well, I guess I'll have to make do with what I've got."

Eiryenne grinned. Leo was going to be so excited when he found out. She knew he'd been dying to go on an outside mission for ages.

They fell silent as horns sounded across the camp.

Both dragon mages sprang to their feet and rushed out the door.

A chill went up Eiryenne's spine. "Intruders already?" she whispered, following them more hesitantly.

Indeed, there were soldiers at the gate. But they weren't wearing the black and silver uniform of the Empire. Their armour varied, from shiny plate armour to orange chainmail and various other combinations. There were elves, Kive, minotaurs, shapeshifters, and other creatures that Eiryenne hadn't seen before. All were bruised and battered, with dented armour and broken lances.

"We have survivors," Lianos muttered.

Danzi nodded. "That explains the tracks I came across." There weren't that many, maybe a few hundred or so. But it was better than nothing.

The warrior at their head raised his hand to silence the chattering that had risen.

"It is my great regret to inform you that Hurraine is dead," he announced.

"Oh, great, it's Jihao," Danzi muttered.

"We are all that remain after a glorious but brutal battle. Our noble leader fell while fighting Varcroft himself and had destroyed fifty hydras before meeting her end. Stabbed in the back, at that," continued the soldier.

"Wrong. Frontal assault by a griffin," the dragon mage said, frowning. "And I don't think Varcroft even has fifty hydras." All those soldiers dead, and the one lieutenant to return had to be Hurraine's poster boy.

Lianos nudged him in the shoulder. "Time for you to go. That's one headache you can really do without."

Danzi sighed. He knew that being confronted by Jihao would only be a waste of time. He turned to Eiryenne. "Get Leo and meet me by the stables in twenty minutes."

She nodded and took off.

Danzi went back into Lianos's cabin, strapping on his sword and putting on his cloak.

Outside, Jihao continued to speak. "We were the only ones valiant enough to survive the onslaught, and I, the most valiant of all, held off ten griffins at once so that my brothers could make it through."

The former leader paused, shaking his head. He'd deal with that nonsense when he got back.

"Therefore, I, Lieutenant Jihao, hereby lay claim to the leadership of the Resistance, as your most worthy candidate..."

Danzi clenched his fists. He could go out there right now and confront the weaselling mage. But that would only gain him two hundred soldiers if he didn't kill half of them during the battle.

Just then Riard rushed into the room. "Well?" he said breathlessly. "What, are you just going to stand there and let him take over?"

"I have my plan," Danzi replied. "And I'm sticking to it. Let Jihao play his little game. It's not as if any one of those soldiers would willingly listen to me right now." Besides, he'd spotted a lot of mages out there. Maybe enough to hold him back. "Now, if you're going to move the camp, as you should, move it here." He handed Riard a piece of paper. "Ridon Point. Defensible on three sides, hard to find, not much space, but it should work."

"What are you going to do?" Riard asked.

Outside, Jihao's speech continued. "… is there none who would object to my reign?"

Danzi smirked. He sent a brilliant burst of red-gold flames whistling up the chimney of the cabin. "I'm going to build an army."

The Adventure Continues In
Dragon's Conquest

About the Author

The author, Arisha Grabtchak, graduated from Dalhousie University with B.Sc. with a double major in Biology and Creative Writing and Honors in Biology in 2015. She self published her first book, Doom of the Teachers when she was 17 in 2011 and distributed it mainly to friends. Writing was her passion. Arisha completed three novels that are parts of the series Red Dragon Chronicles. The novel Dragon Mage is the first one from the series. Arisha also made a few digital drawings related to the story. She was a gifted and multitalented artist creating realistic digital paintings that received high scores from her peers. She was an accomplished scuba diver and a horseback rider. Ocean and horses were her two favorite hobbies. Her plans were very big and ambitious. She shot three short movies in which she acted as a director, an actor and a cameraperson. She dreamed about all her novels to be published and seeing movies based on them. Arisha passed away in 2016 at the age of 23. Her legacy lives in her books that have been published with the support of her family.

www.ingramcontent.com/pod-product-compliance
Lightning Source LLC
Chambersburg PA
CBHW060645260626
47161CB00008B/3012